BEST
LESBIAN
ROMANCE
2014

Edited by

RADCLYFFE

Published in the United States by Cleis Press, Inc., 2246 Sixth Street, Berkeley, California 94710.

Printed in the United States.
Cover design: Scott Idleman/Blink
Cover photograph: Mercè Bellera/Getty Images
Text design: Frank Wiedemann

First Edition.
10 9 8 7 6 5 4 3 2 1

Trade paper ISBN: 978-1-62778-010-0
E-book ISBN: 978-1-62778-023-0

"Sepia Showers" © Andrea Dale, *Love Burns Bright: A Lifetime of Lesbian Romance*, Cleis Press 2013; "The Pond" © D. Jackson Leigh, *Amor and More: Love Everafter*, Bold Strokes Books 2013; "A Sturbridge Idyll" excerpted from *Morton River Valley* © Lee Lynch, Bold Strokes Books, 2013; "Risking It All" © Lynette Mae, *Wild Girls, Wild Nights*, Cleis Press, 2013; "Palabras" © Anna Meadows, *Love Burns Bright: A Lifetime of Lesbian Romance*, Cleis Press 2013.

CONTENTS

BEST
LESBIAN ROMANCE
2014

INTRODUCTION

One thing that makes the romance genre so enduring is the endless variation on the classic "love story." When we begin reading a work of romance, whether it be a short story, a novella or a novel, we already know the ending. Someone will fall in love and hopefully live happily ever after, or at least happily for now. We don't know how they will get there, what challenges they will face or what changes they'll undergo as they cast off old fears, distrust and cynicism to embrace new discoveries and reignited passions. We don't know when they'll finally accept the emotional truth that they've met someone who makes a difference in their life in a way no one else can. We don't know when they'll say the magic words "I love you" and what they'll do after. Every step of a couple's romantic journey is different, in life and in fiction, and the same is true for every story in an anthology about love.

When I put out the call for submissions, I didn't stipulate anything about what constitutes a "romance short story." Like the reader who opens to the first page hoping to discover a story that resonates with their experiences, hopes, dreams and fantasies, I want to be surprised and challenged and inspired by the stories I receive, and the selections in this anthology do not disappoint. What always surprises me is how similar themes converge despite the different voices, different styles and different vantage points of the authors writing romance.

In this collection, completely spontaneously, several themes became apparent—the one that struck me most of all was that of possibility. Romance is a unique and fluid and constantly changing experience, never the same for any two people or even for the same people at different times. But one thing is always true—falling in love opens us up to possibilities we never imagined, leaving us with a deeper sense of self and a greater appreciation for life.

For those at the beginning of the journey, the future is an open road, or as in Sara Rauch's "Current," a swift-moving tide:

> *Clara and I watched the sun descend. It had been a long time since I'd sat like that—with everything and nothing to say. As the thick gashes of magenta and orange striped the horizon, Clara became not a stranger, but a promise.*

For those already on the voyage, love is a source of strength and joy, as Kathleen Tudor writes in "A Boi's Love Song":

> *You give me the courage to be your strong right arm, the bravery to stand between you and the world, wherever I can, and the heart to be proud of everything that I am. By loving me, you show me how much of me there is to love.*

Whatever the path, love is a journey of possibility, passion and promise—enjoy these stories from twenty masters of romance.

Radclyffe
2014

THE GAME OF LOVE

Brittney Loudin

I was in the second semester of my senior year when it happened. If I close my eyes now I can still smell the crisp scent of freshly trimmed grass and the deep musk of hard-earned sweat that never seemed to fade, whether the sport was in season or not. I remember that hot Alabama night so clearly, it replays like a movie in my mind. We were the fashionable subject of gossip, the real talk of the town for months after. Little did I know it would change my life, her life and the perspective of the tiny, rural town forever.

My old teammates and the rest of the student body would tell you differently. Every single one of them would recite his or her own version of the story. Some of their variations would be only partially wrong, simply depicting the major events of the game. Others would narrate complete delusions packed with fabricated details. Regardless of the many different ways the story has been and will be told, only Karen and I know the truth. Only we know what really happened the night a miracle found Southern Crosses High School.

* * *

Coach vehemently kicked at the dirt beneath his sneakers and swore into his clenched fist. He knew better than anyone in that stadium that if he didn't find a perfect replacement and soon, they could kiss the game and their shot at nationals good-bye. It was fourth down and fifteen yards to go until our very own Eagles took the all-state championship. With twenty-one seconds left on the clock, the whole of the spectators were on their feet in the bleachers, gawking with unbelieving eyes as our third wide receiver of the year was hauled off the field by EMTs.

The team had been through hell and back this season but managed to pull off back-to-back wins at the cost of several injured key players. Short four men already and without a quick-footed athlete to run the last play, the team would have no choice but to forfeit.

Standing stationary behind the water cooler, I was the only creature for miles thinking the crazy thought that buzzed between my temples. Any other girl at the school wouldn't have once considered the same solution, but my passion—my passion for the game and my passion for her—ran deeper than all the prejudice the folks in Belmont possessed.

I scanned the corners of the field until my gaze at last landed on the sight I so desperately needed to see, the cheerleaders. In the forefront of the gaggle was the head cheerleader, Karen Peters. I watched as she repeatedly circled the group of glittered-up girls, barking instructions and words of encouragement to those who needed it.

Karen and I had been secretly dating for four months, and as far as I was concerned, she was the sun, the moon, the stars and the very rock of earth beneath my feet. At the young age of seventeen I knew what true love was. I knew what love felt like and looked like because it brought me to my knees every time I saw my own heart reflected in her eyes.

Everybody and their mother could go on for days talking about young love, summer love and even more so, high school sweethearts, but I was fully convinced that what Karen and I had was a love like no other. We connected so easily I couldn't actually recall the first time we met. As far back as my memory stretched, Karen was always there. Best friends for years until conventionality was no longer enough and we had to privately venture into more intimate regions of our relationship to satiate our needs.

She understood me on levels that my peers and family never did. We often stayed up nights, sharing our secret thoughts and dreams, fantasizing about packing up and moving out to New York together, leaving everything and everyone else behind. Karen told me she desperately wanted to become a world-famous dancer, something she wouldn't dare tell her parents, let alone actually do. I divulged the fact that more than anything I wanted to play football in school and then eventually in the NFL. Though my dream was near to impossible, Karen was always a beacon of endless support.

As a matter of fact, it was on one of those days we were babbling on about our hopes and dreams that I asked Karen to marry me. One late afternoon a few weeks prior to the game, we were lying out in her backyard in our swimsuits, chatting away and sipping down pitcher after pitcher of her mama's sweet iced tea. I lifted up my sunglasses and watched her lie there, sprawled out on an old beach towel, trying to steal a tan from overcast clouds.

"Marry you?" She laughed freely into the breeze. "Baby, in this town?" Her Southern twang rode heavily on the back of her innocent treble voice. "People here wouldn't let you wear your hat backward if you wanted to. You know I would tie the knot with you in a heartbeat, baby, but that'll happen the day you win a football game. I'll tell you that."

The day I win a game. Though I knew Karen had used football as a simple comparison to make her point, my brain was saturated with her words. I wanted to play so badly. I wanted *her* so badly.

So when the night of the championship rolled around and the school was in a panic, it was evident to me what I had to do. Nearly paralyzed by the absurdity of my own idea, I forced my feet to shuffle over to the distressed man pacing back and forth on the sideline.

"Coach..." My shaking voice mimicked my trembling hands. "Coach!" Whether he was ignoring my calls or just plumb deep in thought, I couldn't tell. *"Daddy!"*

The man whipped around. "What is it, darlin'? I'm tryin' to run a show here!"

With a hard gulp, I found my words. "Put me in."

"What?"

"Put me in!" My offer now carried the tone of a demand.

He didn't smile but his grimace lost some of its potency and I knew under any less stressful circumstances he would have laughed.

"Ericson, get over here," he shouted to the burly, stocky boy streaming Gatorade into his mouth before turning back to me. "Sweetie, I don't have time for this! I'm gonna pull Ericson from running back and have him make the catch."

"Daddy, you know he can't make it. He's not fast enough. He doesn't even know the play that well!"

"I don't have a choice, honey."

"Yes, you do. *Me.* I know it. I know that play better than any of those meatheads. You know I can, you've seen me run it a million times."

To this day I have never seen such desperation in my father's eyes as I did that night while he stood there staring down at me, silently weighing his longing for the win and his pre-programmed mentality that told him no girl would ever, could ever, be good enough to really play.

Ericson finally trotted over to my side, beads of sweat flying from his forehead. "Yeah, Coach?" With a gathered brow, my father's regard hung on me a moment longer and then he turned to the boy. "Get your helmet. Then take your shoulder pads and jersey off and give them to Jane here."

With confusion, the young man acquiesced.

"Two minutes, kid," he ordered before spitting in the grass and walking off.

I donned the pads like they were pieces of armor and I was preparing for battle. After slipping the jersey, stained green and brown, over my head, I snatched the oversized helmet from its seat on the bench and made my descent onto the field.

The murmurs of the crowd swelled into a bellowing roar as they slowly recognized my smaller frame jogging toward the nest of bewildered players waiting for Coach's orders.

I whistled sharply and when I had the team's undivided attention I signed the code for the play and motioned for them to get into form. Not one boy commented or argued with my self-appointed authority. I'm sure that any other day of the week I would have been blown back by snide remarks and sexist jests, but the energy in the air that night was far too intense for jokes. I had often practiced with the boys during off seasons and my competence wasn't in question. For one evening our mutual desire put us on the same level. We were one team.

Squatting into our designated positions, we waited for the opposing team to follow suit. The fire building in my gut evaporated all my anxieties. This was it. This was the moment I had envisioned since childhood.

With a final glance over at Karen's concerned face across the field, I shut my eyes and knelt to touch the grass, securing my hunched stance. The stadium was silent apart from the banging sound of my heart floundering about underneath the pads and the nasal wheezing of my accelerated breath.

The call was made and within seconds my feet were a blur under my body as I bolted toward the goalpost. Dashing into the end zone, I twisted my torso back and checked the air. Sure enough, the ball was hurtling right for my head. Kicking hard off the ground, I leapt into the air, throwing my arms as wide as I possibly could. I grabbed the ball, cradling it into my chest as I fell to the dirt.

The referee's whistle couldn't be heard over the audience's cheers. Still grasping the ball for dear life, I stood and saw my teammates pouncing on one another, beating on their chests and howling with excitement. Then it hit me. We won. I had been so overwhelmed by the fact that I was playing in a real game I had forgotten all about the possible outcome.

When I felt arms swing around my neck, I thought they belonged to another player reveling in the victory, but then I saw Karen. Her ear-to-ear smile melted my racing heart. She was beyond elated.

Unable to contain her bliss, she screamed, "Baby, you did it! We won the championship and you did it." She was literally jumping for joy.

I tossed my helmet on the ground, and in a moment of unadulterated euphoria, grabbed Karen by her waist and picked her up, allowing her to snake her tan, lean legs around my hips. Looking into each other's eyes, we both knew it wasn't really me. It was fate.

"The day I win a game, right?" My lips lightly brushed her cheek and my chest heaved from loss of breath. "I do believe you owe me a wedding, ma'am."

Karen discarded her rattling pom-poms and weaved her fingers through the cropped, damp, clustered hair sticking to my face. "Let's do it, baby. Jane Adams, let's leave and I will marry you tonight, tomorrow night or any night you want. I'm yours. I love you, baby."

"I love you, too." With that, I kissed Karen hard on her lips, right smack-dab in the middle of the end zone. I didn't care that all of Belmont was watching. I didn't care if her daddy would shoot me or hell, if my own daddy would shoot me. If that night proved anything, it was that Karen and I were destined, written in the stars, and we both knew it. It was all we talked about on the flight to New York, graduation night.

THE THINGS YOU DON'T DO

Jane Fletcher

"Tell my daughter to get her sweet butt in here. I haven't paid for all this so she can sulk off on her own."

"Yes sir." Annie O'Donnell, the maid, bobbed a curtsy and scuttled away.

She spared a cursory glance for the room. The party was in full swing. Everyone in the district with pretensions to being considered high society had tried to wrangle an invite. The ballroom was crowded with bright young things. Admittedly not all were young, and some were most definitely not bright. "Things" was, though, a sufficiently generous category to include everyone there, with just a few regrettable exceptions.

The music from the jazz quartet overlaid the hubbub of two hundred voices. Scents from numerous bouquets, decorating the edges of the room, battled with that of expensive perfume, cigarette smoke and, increasingly, alcohol on the revelers' breaths. The light from three huge crystal chandeliers glittered off jewelry, necklaces, cufflinks and even a couple of tiaras. Above the band hung a banner, embroidered with the words, *Happy 21st Birthday, Beth.*

The men present were mostly dressed conventionally with crisp white shirts and tails. Annie had seen the table by the entrance piled high with top hats. The women wore a mixture of elegant evening gowns, small black dresses and even smaller tubes of bright material, in the latest fashion, cut so short the wearer's knees were on show. These dresses were mainly the preserve of younger women, accompanied by headbands (and the occasional feather) and strings of heavy beads. Black-clad waiters wove their way between the crowds, carrying trays heavily laden with pink champagne.

At that moment the band struck up a Charleston and the knees jostled onto the dance floor to commence their gyrations. Annie left the room. She knew the birthday girl would not be among them.

The entrance hall of the Fitzpatrick mansion was larger than the entire apartment Annie shared with her aunt, uncle and five young cousins. A wide sweep of stairs led to the upper floor. She hesitated briefly. The young lady of the household might be up there, taking refuge in her room, but then Annie shook her head. No. She had a better idea of where to find Miss Elizabeth Fitzpatrick.

The double doorway at the rear of the hall stood open, giving access to the garden. The cool night air was a welcome change from the heavy, too sweet atmosphere inside. Lanterns had been set around the terrace. Their flames flickered in the gentle breeze blowing in from the sea. Beyond the stone balustrade, moonlight bleached the garden in harsh blue-white light and soft black shadows. Still farther away, the distant lights of the city reflected in the black waters of the bay.

Annie was not the only one on the terrace. A few others had

drifted out to enjoy the night air. They stood talking quietly in pairs and trios. Red lights flickered like fireflies as people drew on their cigarettes. A sudden burst of laughter, quickly hushed, caught Annie's attention. She looked over, but her quarry was not there—nor had Annie expected it. She knew where to look.

Stairs at either end of the terrace led down to the garden. The sound of Annie's footsteps changed from the sharp click of stone to the crunch of loose gravel. As she walked down the path, the sounds of the party faded and gave way to the song of crickets and the whisper of wind through the bushes. At first no more than a faint undercurrent, but growing louder, was the boom of the sea washing against the bottom of the cliffs. Annie took a deep breath, expelling the last of the smoke and alcohol fumes from her lungs.

At the end of the lawn the path passed between a pair of topiary bushes in the shape of peacocks before rounding a now-silent fountain. Beyond lay the less formal area of the garden, degenerating into an overgrown rockery. The path no longer ran straight. After another minute, it ended at a promontory where an old, round wooden summerhouse overlooked the ocean. The building appeared deserted in the brilliant moonlight, but Annie had little doubt of who would be there.

She stopped in the doorway, letting her eyes adjust to the darkness inside. Sitting to one side was the heir to the Fitzpatrick shipping fortune. A stray beam of moonlight glinted off the shimmering silver evening dress clinging to her slender form.

"Your father sent me to find you, Miss Elizabeth."

"Well, please don't tell him you found me, and please don't call me Elizabeth."

The rich, warm voice made Annie's insides melt. Before trusting herself to reply, she took a second to ensure she had full control of her lungs. "Lizzie." The name felt more stilted on her lips than it used to.

"Annie."

Even without seeing her face, by the lilt in Lizzie's tone, Annie knew she was smiling. Just the memory of that smile was enough to make Annie's pulse leap and her knees weaken. She leaned against the door frame for support.

"Can you do me a favor? Go back to the party and get me a glass of bubbly." Lizzie paused, reflectively. "Actually, make that two, and see if you can snag a bottle as well."

"Supposing I meet with your father, what will I say?"

"What exactly did Daddy ask you to do?"

Annie searched her memory. "To tell you to get your sweet butt into the party."

"Consider me told." Lizzie laughed. "If you see him, you don't have to lie. You can say you couldn't find me in the house. Which is true. And you can say you're going to try find me in the garden. You don't need to add that since you know where I am, your chances of finding me are extremely good."

Annie shook her head, in amusement rather than denial. If truth be told, she would have lied for Lizzie, willingly.

Back in the house, the party was, if anything, even more exuberant than before. The absence of the birthday girl did not appear to be hampering the proceedings to any noticeable degree. A few young men were wandering around as if in a very halfhearted game of hunt the parcel, but even they seemed more interested in the champagne.

Annie did not run into Mr. Fitzpatrick, so was spared the need to be inventive with the truth. No one else paid her any attention, the black maid's uniform rendering her invisible, unless she was carrying drinks. Unfortunately, this was the fate suffered the first four glasses of champagne she acquired, but she was eventually able to get away safely, drinks and bottle in hand.

By the time she returned to the summerhouse, the moon had moved on, and now enough beams reached the interior for her to see Lizzie's face, highlighting the plains of her fine high cheekbones and small upturned nose. The colors Annie had to provide from memory, the gold in the ringlets of Lizzie's hair and her cornflower blue eyes.

Annie handed over a glass of champagne and looked around, wondering where to place the other. A bench ran the full circumference of the walls, but it was not level enough to stand the glass on without risk, and there was no table. She bent, about to place the second drink and the open bottle on the floor by Lizzie's feet.

"No. That one's for you."

Annie placed a hand on the ground for balance and looked up, uncertain. "I don't..."

"Oh, for god's sake, Annie, sit down and drink it. I want to ask your advice."

"Why me?"

"Because I trust you and you know me better than anyone else. Like you're the only one who knows I can't stand Beth and prefer to be called Lizzie. Now sit down."

Annie did as she was told, taking a safe position at the other side of the summerhouse, and sipped the champagne. The bubbles tickled her nose. "What are you wanting advice about?"

"Daddy's given me an ultimatum."

"Another?"

"He's serious this time. I have to get married." Lizzie gave a humorless laugh. "He's even given me a schedule. I've got my choice of the young bucks here tonight, with a view to announcing our engagement within six months. I'm to be married by next

Christmas, and he went as far as to hint at a grandchild by the end of the following year."

"You're wanting to know how to wriggle out of it."

Lizzie laughed and pointed the now half-empty glass at Annie. "That's why I'm asking you. Do you know, any of my friends would have assumed I wanted advice about which man to pick." She tilted her head to one side, appraising Annie. "You really do know me. We used to be close."

"We used to be children."

"True. Growing up isn't all it's made out to be."

Annie smiled, slightly sadly. In truth, it had all been so much easier when they were children. She had started work at the Fitzpatricks' straight off the boat from Ireland and needed to lie about her age to qualify for employment. It had been such a strange new world she found herself in.

Lizzie had been a scant year younger than herself, equally lost. Her mother, Margaret Fitzpatrick, had succumbed to cancer a few months earlier. Notwithstanding their difference in station, they had become friends, supporting each other as they adjusted to their new situations. At the time, it had felt like being sisters. But as they became older, things had become more complex. Things always do. The way Annie now felt about Lizzie was not an iota less affectionate, but it could not be described as sisterly.

When Lizzie had been sent to finishing school in Switzerland, Annie had tried telling herself it was a blessing. She would be spared the daily torment of seeing Lizzie and the fight to keep her words and actions under control. But being around Lizzie had been the sweetest of torments, and her life had been so very empty without her, so lacking in joy.

With each passing month, Annie had told herself she was coming to terms with her feelings and was over the worst of it.

She had been lying to herself. Deep inside she had known it all along, and if she hadn't then, she would now, sitting alone with Lizzie in the dark summerhouse.

Lizzie had returned from Switzerland a month ago—a month that had passed at a hectic pace, catching up with old school friends and the like. Lizzie had spent more time out of the house than in it. Again Annie had lied to herself, saying they were adults, with utterly separate lives, and she did not want, and certainly did not expect, anything else. This meeting in the summerhouse was the first time they had exchanged more than a sentence and already the thin shell of self-deception was melting, like ice in a blast furnace. She had missed Lizzie, like a drowning man misses oxygen.

Annie felt her pulse race and her stomach tightened in a knot. Her mouth grew dry. She took a quick gulp of champagne. Unwise. Already she could feel the first faint blurring of alcohol. She put the glass down. Keeping her head clear was vital. "Why do you think your father is so much more serious this time?"

"Because he spent money on this party. Daddy never spends money unless he's serious."

"What will happen if you refuse?"

"He's threatened to cut off my allowance."

"Do you think he will?"

Lizzie shrugged by way of answer.

"So what options do you have?"

Lizzie drained her glass and got to her feet. Annie's heart jumped at the thought Lizzie was coming to sit beside her, but instead she stood in the doorway of the summerhouse, resting her shoulder on the frame, her back to Annie and stared out across the bay.

"Europe was wonderful. Not the school. That was a waste of time. Nothing of value, except I can now say *ooh la la* and *la dolce vita,* which passes for sophistication around here, so Daddy's pleased. But the places…"

Lizzie turned and rested her back against the door frame. Her gaze fixed on the ceiling, but Annie had the sense she wasn't seeing it. Her mind's eye was fixed on other scenes, other times. Annie waited for Lizzie to speak again.

"Europe's nothing like here—the buildings, the people. The world is filled with so many places I want to see. Places I have to see." Her eyes dropped, fixing on Annie. "Do you remember my camera?"

"Of course." How could she forget it?

The camera had been a present for Lizzie's fifteenth birthday. For the following two years, they had done nothing except play with this new toy. Lizzie had talked her father into equipping a small darkroom. Standing cramped together, in the dark, Annie had first begun to realize just how her feelings for Lizzie were changing, and what she wanted. And then everything had all become just too difficult.

The camera had not been a fad. Lizzie carried it everywhere with her. The cupboard in one of the spare rooms was filled with boxes upon boxes of photographs. Nor had Annie's new understanding of herself been a fad. But in her case, it was her heart that was filled, with memory upon memory, and hopeless dreams.

Lizzie continued. "During the summer break they took us on the grand tour. France, Italy, Greece, the lot. It was supposed to make us cultured. But I have to tell you, some of the girls I was with, it was a complete lost cause. We went to Naples. The other girls who had cameras took snaps of Pompeii."

"And you didn't?"

"I gave the chaperones the slip one afternoon and wandered around downtown Naples. There was a fruit market. That's what I photographed. Old women arguing over cabbages. Young men carrying barrels. A boy crouched down, peeking between a donkey's legs. A baby sleeping in a makeshift crib sculpted from sacks of oranges."

Annie couldn't help but smile. "That sounds like you. Never doing what everyone else does. Do you have the photographs with you? I'd like to see them."

"I've got a few prints, but I sold the negatives."

"You sold them? Who to?"

"A magazine." Lizzie's tone gained a sharp edge of excitement and possibly pride. "It's the first money I've ever made for myself."

Things were becoming clearer, and Annie could guess where they were heading. "How long could you live on it?"

"Oh, not long at all. But the magazine said if I had other photographs, they'd like to see them."

"You're thinking you can make a career of it?"

"I don't know. For the last year, I've been putting aside some money from my allowance. Daddy doesn't know. It'll see me through a short while, but beyond that..." She sighed. "I don't know. I really don't know."

"And this is what you're wanting my advice about?"

"Yes, Annie. What would you do if you were me?"

Wisdom be damned. Annie took a large mouthful of champagne, and then another. If Lizzie went, if she never saw her again, could she bear it? But how could she be less than fair? And what hope was there, even if Lizzie stayed? Either way, her own case was hopeless, but at least she could know she had been honest, she had been true. And at least one of them could be happy.

"For me, coming to America was a big step. But what with me Da not coming home from the war and me Ma with too many mouths to feed, there was nothing for me in Ireland. My aunt gave me the chance to come over with her, but I didn't know what to do. So I asked my Gran, and you know what she said?"

Lizzie tilted her head to one side. The rhetorical question needed no answer.

"She said, in life it's the things you don't do you end up regretting the most. And my Gran was right. Life has been better for me here. I'd have been a fool to stay behind."

"You think I should give the photography a go?"

"Yes. And I don't think you've much to lose. Even if it doesn't work out, if you came back with your tail between your legs I'm betting your father would welcome you back with open arms, just to show he'd been right all along."

"But could I bear to give him that satisfaction?" Despite her words, Lizzie sounded happier.

"Then don't fail."

Lizzie's answer was no more than the softest of laughs. Her body relaxed and her head dropped. For a long time she stayed in place. Clearly her thoughts moved to something else. At last she drew a deep breath and raised her head. "There's one more thing."

"What?"

Instead of answering, Lizzie left the doorway and picked up the bottle to refill her glass. For a moment it looked as if she would reoccupy her previous spot, but after two hesitant half steps, first one way, and then the other, she crossed the summerhouse and threw herself down on the bench next to Annie, so close their knees were almost touching. Annie felt the tension flare up inside, her skin at the same time too hot yet icy cold. What more could there be? She clasped her hands together around her glass, frightened they would reach out of their own accord.

Lizzie held out the bottle. "You're empty."

Annie let her fill the glass, fighting so the trembling of her hands did not betray her. She risked a sideways glance. Lizzie was concentrating on the task, her lips pursed in concentration—like a kiss. When Lizzie leaned to put the bottle on the ground, Annie quickly looked away, before their eyes could meet.

"The places I'll be traveling, they're not always safe for a woman to go alone. Well, to be honest, they're not too safe for anyone, sometimes. And I've got all my photographic equipment to carry, and I was wondering..."

Heart in mouth, Annie waited for Lizzie to continue. Normally, she might guess where Lizzie's words were heading, but in taking the next step, were her own dreams feeding her false hope? When no more came, Annie gathered her courage, to finish the sentence, trying to pitch her voice so she could pass it off as a joke, if need be. "Are you saying you want someone to help carry your bags?"

Lizzie smiled in response, but the set of her lips was less confident than normal. "I wouldn't put it quite like that. I want a companion, an assistant. Someone who can help me. Someone a bit more practical than me, and a bit more worldly wise." She paused, staring down at her own hands, but then looked up. "Would you be willing to come with me, Annie?"

Annie felt her heart pound again, more fiercely than at any time that evening. It roared in her ears, but not loud enough to drown out, softly through the intervening years, her Gran's voice and the advice she gave. *It's the things you don't do you end up regretting the most.*

Dare she say yes? If she did, how would she bear the months ahead, with Lizzie so close yet out of reach? But how could she live with herself if she didn't? Annie's mouth was painfully dry. Yet she drained her drink more in hope of summoning Dutch courage than for the sake of easing it. She put down the glass and faced Lizzie.

"I'll come with you on one condition."

"What's that?"

Annie slid along the bench so their legs were in contact from knee to thigh. She was close enough to see the moonlight reflecting in Lizzie's eyes, hear her breathe, smell the perfume on her skin and the alcohol on her breath. Close enough to see the pulse beating in Lizzie's throat.

"That you ask me again in one minute's time."

"What do you think is going to happen in the next minute to change my mind?"

"This."

It was too late to debate the wisdom. Closing her eyes, Annie leaned forward. Her lips brushed softly against Lizzie's before returning again, hard.

At the first touch, Lizzie flinched, but did not pull away. Her face and lips were frozen, possibly in outrage—Annie dared not open her eyes to see. Then Lizzie's hand rose to Annie's face. At first it seemed as if she was preparing to push Annie away, or slap her, but instead, at the last moment, it slipped behind Annie neck, pulling them yet closer. Their lips molded together.

It was the kiss Annie had fantasized about for years. The kiss that had haunted her dreams and tormented her days. This was what she wanted from Lizzie—wanted with all her heart and soul. She wrapped her arms around Lizzie, hugging her close. The solidity of Lizzie's body against hers filled a gaping hole in her heart. If nothing else in her life ever went right, this was the moment she would draw on for the rest of her days, the moment that made living her life worthwhile.

At last they broke apart, both breathing deeply. Lizzie raised her hand to her mouth, as if to reassure herself that her lips were still her own. Her expression flitted between confusion, uncertainty and surprise. She stared at her fingers with the bewilderment of someone expecting to see something new and strange imprinted there, and then her eyes lifted to meet Annie's. Slowly the confusion faded, replaced by the softest of smiles.

"Annie O'Donnell, will you run away with me?"

PALABRAS

Anna Meadows

The only secret I ever kept from Sawyer fit inside an orange crate.

She almost found it once, the day we moved in together. I had buried it in the backseat of my car, beneath my great-aunt's quilts and the box that held my mixing bowls. When I saw Sawyer come up the stairs with that wooden crate my grandfather had painted the cobalt of a blue glass jar, my heart was tight as a knot in cherry wood.

I told her that the things inside had belonged to my grandfather, that I kept them only because they smelled like him, like the cardamom of his favorite *tortas* and the loose tobacco he rolled into paper. They would mean nothing to me if it weren't for that, I told her. It could have been anything, I said, as long as it held that same spice and earth.

She believed me. They always believe you if you want it enough.

And it wasn't all a lie. Everything in that crate my grandfather gave me, and every time I took it down from the top of the closet, the whole apartment smelled like my grandmother's *pan de muerto*. That's why I never took it down unless I knew there was enough time to let that perfume slip out the open windows before Sawyer got home. The few times I spent so long fingering its contents that the scent was too heavy to dissipate, I made *tortas de aceite* with enough cardamom that Sawyer didn't notice.

Sometimes I longed to show her everything in that orange crate, to spill its contents onto our bed and give over its secrets. But I didn't want to lose her. "Never let the boy think you are smarter than he is, *m'ija*," my mother told me. "You never keep him if he thinks you're smart." When I met Sawyer, I thought the same went for a woman who dressed like a boy.

My mother hated that my grandfather gave me so many books. He told me I was smart and that if I did not read enough I would get lonely. "You want to know things," he said. He could tell by the ring of blue-black around the brown of my irises. So he brought me a book each time he came to visit. One month a book of Irish poets who sang of a land so green it broke their hearts open. Another, a dictionary, because whenever I asked my mother what a word meant she said, "You ask so many questions, you stop being pretty one day," and told me to stir the Spanish rice. For my birthday, a hardcover about the birds of the cloud forests where he met my grandmother. Its glossy pages shined with the emerald of hummingbirds and the blue tourmaline of the *quetzal*'s tail feathers.

He had brought me books for two years when my mother told me I was getting too smart. "No boy likes you if you talk like that," she said. *"Todas aquellas palabras."* All those words. It was two months before my thirteenth birthday, and she bleached my hair to the yellow of the *masa* we used for tamales.

She said making me blonde would make up for all those books because my hair would keep boys from seeing those rings of midnight blue around my eyes.

Even after my grandfather was gone, my mother kept dyeing my hair. When I moved out, I did it myself, a force of habit as strong as biting my nails or reading *la Biblia* before bed. I knew she was right. I needed the maize-gold of my hair to hide what my grandfather had seen. He might have loved me for it, but no boy would.

When I moved in with Sawyer, I had to get rid of most of my grandfather's books. I could only keep as many as I could hide. Choosing which would stay was harder than picking which doll and which two dresses to take with me when I was a little girl and my family had to evacuate for the canyon fires. It was harder than how I never opened my eyes all the way in front of Sawyer, afraid she'd see those rings of blue. She always thought it was how I flirted with her, half closing my eyes like that.

A book about chaos theory had taught me that a butterfly flitting its wings at just the right time off the coast of my *abuela*'s hometown in Guatemala could turn the tide of the Mediterranean Sea. It sounded so much like a fairy tale, that little winged creature pulling on the oceans as much as the moon, that I grew drunk off dreams of *las mariposas* and a million coins of water. It had to come with me.

A small paperback, a French children's book about a boy who loved a rose so much it lit all the stars for him, more than earned the sliver of space it took up in the orange crate. The corners of a picture guide to the wildflowers of North America were still soft from my grandfather's thumbs, so I kept it. I held on to a hardcover of Neruda's poems if only for the line, "I do not love you as if you were salt-rose or topaz."

Books would not have been such a secret for most women.

They would have slid them onto the same shelves with their lovers', letting the spines mix until they could not have remembered whose began as whose if not for the names written onto the flyleaves. But I never forgot my mother telling me, "Never let the boy think you are smart." Sawyer loved me for my push-up bras and rosewater perfume, my cayenne-colored lipstick and all that yellow hair I made endless with hot rollers each morning. It didn't matter that by the time we'd been together for three years, she knew I dyed it.

I loved Sawyer for her saffron-colored hair, always just long enough to get in her eyes. I loved her for how the weight of the Leatherman on her belt pulled her jeans just enough to show a band of bare skin at the small of her back. I loved that her tongue always tasted like saltwater.

I loved these things about her the way she loved those things about me, so it was not fair to let her know I was curious and smart like my grandfather had told me. It would have changed too much. It would have made her doubt the way I laughed when she traced a finger along the scalloped lace of my bra, or how, after I ironed her shirts, I liked leaving a blush of lipstick on those clean, starched collars. All of that was true. All of it was as much me as the secrets inside that orange crate. But Sawyer might not have believed it. My mother might have been right about all my words.

Sawyer had loved me that way for seven years when I came home and found her with my grandfather's books. It was the weekend after Thanksgiving. She'd taken down the Christmas decorations from the high shelf of the closet and had found my orange crate behind the boxes.

"I wanted to surprise you," she said. She bit her lip, a little guilty. "Thought I could get all the lights up before you came home."

I blushed to see that the books were in a different order than when I had last put them back in the crate. Sawyer had gone through them.

She caught me staring. "Sorry," she said. "I didn't mean to go looking where you didn't want me to."

"I don't care," I said. "They're just books. I never read them."

"Then why's your handwriting in them?"

I knelt on the floor to put them all back in the right order, but Sawyer took my face in her hands. I felt the familiar grain of her calluses on my cheeks, the pads of her fingers worn rougher since the first time she touched me years earlier.

"You're smart," she said, her mouth close enough to mine that I could feel its heat on my lips. "I see it."

I loved my lipstick and my rosewater as much as *todas aquellas palabras,* and I loved Sawyer more than any of it. I wanted both. I wanted my body to be soft under hers, not so full of words that I was as hard to hold in her arms as water.

But she held me a little harder, her calluses like the finest sandpaper. I imagined each of her fingertips on my tongue, rough and sweet as the husks of the lychee nuts we bought from the farmer's market on Sunday mornings. Thinking of how much the fruit inside smelled like violets on our sheets made me close my eyes. A tear fell from my lash line.

Sawyer kissed it when it was halfway down my cheek. "What else are you hiding?" she asked.

I opened my eyes and let her look at me. I did not squint to keep from her those rings around the brown of my irises. She stared into me like I was fire opal, and I knew she'd seen them, that deep blue that had first told my grandfather I was a girl for questions and words, all those words.

"Did you think I didn't know?" Sawyer asked.

She put her hands on my waist and kissed me, quickly but gently, like she was pinning me down. She wanted me, still touched me like I was as soft as wet roses, even with all those secret pages. I was a butterfly over the waters of my grandmother's homeland, and Sawyer was an ocean I could move with the flicker of my eyelashes, as easily as if they were wings.

My hand found that band of bare skin between her shirt and her jeans. My fingers brushed the knobs of her spine. The soft whistle of her breath in through her teeth gave me permission to pull her shirt away from the warmth of her back, and then her body was as open as the Ireland of those poets. Her tongue, her breasts, her thighs were salt-rose and topaz on my lips. She had irises as green as those cloud forest hummingbirds, and the black in the center of each opened and spread when she slid her hand up my skirt.

She reached between my thighs like I was her rose and she was that boy who loved me like a sky's worth of stars. She touched me like I was all petals, her fingers looking for the tight bud at the center.

She was all those words. *Todas aquellas palabras.* And I could tell her all of it, everything, as soon as I caught my breath.

CURRENT

Sara Rauch

I emerged from the upstairs bathroom, having gone in twenty minutes before to cry my eyes out. I'd redrawn my liner and lashes from Poppy's makeup bag, but I still felt shitty, was thinking of slipping out the side door through the yard and running for home. Clara caught me off guard. She was there at the top of the stairs, waiting. I jumped and said, "Shit." I was past polite, past profound. I knew my eyes were puffy and bloodshot despite the freshly applied kohl.

"Sorry," she said. "I saw you come up here and—"

I studied her, her outfit and unfamiliar face. I'd glimpsed her downstairs, sitting by the window alone, beer in hand. She had a nose pointy like a woodpecker, and a crest of dark blond hair, pale skin, shadowy smudges beneath her light blue eyes. All I could manage was, "Oh?"

She said, "I wanted to talk to you. Now that I'm standing here, it seems like I'm being strange."

It did seem strange, but I'd been crying in the bathroom at an afternoon potluck, wishing my ex was dead and not my dad, and it was one of those floating September afternoons that always got under my skin. My thirty-second birthday was a week away. My mother had sent a ring—she rarely visited, though I'd asked her to many times—a thick band set with rubies, and a note that read: *This is your year for peace and passion.* My mother was a gemologist, so I figured this arcane blessing had something to do with the stones. I rarely wore jewelry, but I wore the ring that afternoon, constantly aware of its weight on my finger.

"No, not strange. I just wasn't expecting you," I said.

Clara stepped toward me and touched my arm. She said, "I'm Clara. I work with Dale at the university." There was something in Clara's face, some openness, that made her proximity, her assertiveness comforting rather than grating.

"Sienna," I said. "Poppy's best friend."

For many weeks I'd had the feeling that I was approaching a cliff, with no idea of what came next, with no parachute or brakes. All the desire I once carried—to be an artist, to do something with my life, to make meaningful contact with another human being—had come to naught. I carried with me, instead, an unbearable sense of loneliness.

"Why're you hiding out up here?" Clara asked.

"Avoiding my ex."

Dale and Poppy's parties were legendary. Today the crowded rooms of their immaculate house and the people in bright colors dappled across the back lawn merely added to my sense of removal. How unlike my best friend I was, with her perfect hostess skills. But like always, I'd come early, in my black jersey dress, to help her set up. To listen to Poppy gossip about the hook-ups and breakups of our mutual acquaintances and several couples I'd met at other parties. What Poppy seemed to be saying today was that nothing was wrong with me at all—relationships blossomed and they shed their petals, the cycles of life, blah-blah. At least she was kind enough not to point out that it'd been many years since she'd seen me in bloom.

"Your ex is here?" Clara asked, biting her lip.

"The cocky brunette. Nancy."

Clara shook her head, which I took to mean she didn't know who I was talking about. Nancy was visiting from the West Coast, that's why Poppy invited her. *You don't mind, do you?* Poppy had asked, putting a baking sheet of biscuits into the oven. *It's been seven years,* I'd said and was happy that Poppy couldn't see my face. The worst part was I knew I shouldn't mind. It'd been forever. And it hadn't been that great anyway. Nancy was self-absorbed and bad in bed.

"One great thing about moving a lot," Clara said. "No need to confront your past at parties."

"Are you new to town?" I asked.

"Two years." She pushed her hands through her hair, letting the little pomp on the front fall back against her forehead.

"I've been in the Valley since college," I said. "Fourteen long years."

"You don't like it?"

"I do, I just wish—I don't know. For something new. New air."

"It's overrated."

"What is?"

"New air."

I looked down the stairs to the glass sliding door that opened out onto the patio. There was Nancy's back, and the lit-up face of Poppy's friend Annabelle. They were drinking martinis and leaning in close to one another. I felt the warmth of Clara's arm near mine, the little blond hairs tickling me.

I stood, not steadily, and said, "I need to get outta here."

Clara said, "Do you want to go to my place? It isn't far."
Under any other circumstance I would have said no. But that
afternoon did not feel normal. I felt like a fish that had suddenly
grown legs, or a human waking to a set of gills—unsure of what
to do with myself, afraid of the strange gift I'd been given.
I said sure. I motioned to Clara to follow me, and we slipped
out the side door by the downstairs bathroom. Walking across
the lawn, the grass long and lush and tickling my ankles, I felt
a moment of urgency pass through me. I stopped abruptly and
turned. Clara, not paying attention, almost crashed into me.

I said, my voice quiet though I knew it didn't matter, "I wonder
how long it'll be till they notice we're gone?" And I giggled. The
sound was foreign as it emerged from my mouth and filled the
air. Clara raised her eyebrows and gave a sly smile.

"Maybe never," she said, and I hoped she was right.

She whistled at the old maroon Volvo. I dug in my purse
for my keys and when I unearthed them, she closed her hand
around mine. "Could I drive? I love these old cars," she said.

"Where's your car?" I asked, confused.

"I don't have one."

"How'd you get here?"

"I walked," she said.

I never let anyone drive my car. The old Volvo's clutch was
loose and it frequently ground between gears or stalled out in
second if it wasn't given the proper finesse. It had been my dad's
before he died.

Maybe it was her hand around mine. Maybe it was the dying
of another summer. Maybe it was the feeling of a petal or two
loosening from the bud. I gave her the keys. She got in and leaned
across the seat to pop open the door. She said, "Get in." Coming
from anyone else it would have seemed a command, but from
her, it was gentle. Most everything about her was gentle.

All I really knew about her was that she worked with Dale (which department, had she said?) and that she lived on Wood Street and dressed like a dandy. Or at least, she had for the party we were leaving—pressed gray trousers and matching vest, a burgundy tie knotted over a white short-sleeved oxford.

I'd never been to Wood Street, in fact had no idea where it was. It wasn't like Northampton was a small town, but having been around for so many years, I figured I knew all the streets, neighborhoods, places to see or be seen. Wood Street, Clara told me, was at the edge of town, out by the highway.

It was only a few miles, but Clara took the long way, down the narrow back streets, turning right and left and left again. Her pants pulled taut over her legs as she worked the pedals— she was slender but solid, I could see the muscles in her thighs flex as she pressed the clutch—and her spoon-shaped fingers manipulated the gearshift with ease.

Stopped at a red light, she glanced over at me. Autumn hadn't peeled back summer's warmth, though September was almost finished, and we drove with the windows down, my arm extended and hand gliding the air currents. Poppy would wonder where I was when the party ended, but that was several hours away. She liked to recap the minutiae as she cleared dirty glasses and loaded the dishwasher. It was her favorite part of the party, or at least one of them. Her sweet round face would be flushed with more gossip, recounting the silly moments—*Did you see Max hit Greg with the croquet mallet? Priceless*—who'd been drunk and who'd not shown.

Clara and I drove past pastel Victorians and farmhouses with sagging front porches. She drove slowly, as if relishing each turn the wheel made, each time she downshifted. I stared out the window, saw my reflection in the side mirror—dark hair lifting in the breeze, the sharp curve of my nose. The streets became unfamiliar, the houses and yards shabbier.

I lived near the college, in the opposite direction from which we were headed, in a second-floor apartment with refurbished wood floors and drafty windows. The apartment, beautiful and spacious, cost more than half my monthly income at the food safety nonprofit where I worked, but I'd reasoned it was worth it—given the location. I could walk to cafés and bars, there was a meticulous park only a few blocks away. Years ago, when I'd signed the lease, I'd reasoned that was enough. Now it loomed as a symbol of my inadequacy—sterile and stagnant.

As we got closer to the highway, she said, "I have a cat. You aren't allergic, are you?"

"No," I said. "I have a cat too. Laurent."

"Mine's Bell."

"Like the translator."

She looked at me as if I'd unintentionally caught her naked. Then she looked forward again, smiling. "Yeah, like the translator." Her teeth were remarkably white but very crooked, both incisors jutting over the teeth in front of them.

She pulled up to the curb in front of a small white house with white shutters. She eased the gearshift into neutral, sliding it back and forth a few times before killing the engine. Noise from the highway filled the air: steel rushing, the peculiar long whine of cars passing through, the occasional horn or tractor trailer, the dissonance of movement.

"Here we are," she said.

I sat staring at the house until she reached across me and opened the passenger door. She didn't touch me, but her arm so close to my chest made me hold my breath. I was suddenly afraid, as if the gills I'd imagined growing earlier could suck in air because of Clara's presence.

Clara got out of the car and waited for me to do the same

before locking it with the key. Most people didn't know that was how to lock those old Volvos, that just pushing down the button inside the door did nothing. She handed me the keys and we went up the walkway together.

"You have a house, but not a car," I said. Agitation and desire bubbled in me.

"A fair trade, don't you think?" she said.

She opened the front door, letting me enter before her, and I was about to turn, about to say *I have to go,* because I wanted to go, wanted to put space between me and this woman I barely knew, whose hand was on the small of my back sending spark waves through my body, when I noticed the white. It was hard not to. Everything in the small front room was painted white. Not ivory, not cream. Pure white, straight from the can. The only furniture in the room was an overstuffed white chair, atop which sat a small white cat. Bell. She meowed and jumped down and ran into the house.

Fascination short-circuited my nervousness and pulled me farther inside. I followed Clara from room to room. Each yielded more white—floors, baseboards and molding, the entire bathroom, the bedspread and curtains and mirror frames. There were occasional splashes of color—a squat, curvy aqua-color vase on a little shelf, a deep purple throw over the end of the bed—but everything else was white. And there wasn't much of anything. Entire rooms were empty. Probably every piece of furniture in the house would have fit into her bedroom, which was not particularly large. I tried to think of something to say, but only inane sentences—*You like white*—came to mind. I kept quiet and tried to not let my mind run over with anxiety. We passed a door with a small square cut from the bottom—*The basement,* Clara said. Was the basement also white? I wondered. It was better not to know.

In the kitchen, the last stop on the tour, everything, as I expected it to be, was white. The refrigerator, the stove, the countertop and linoleum, the dishes sitting on the open shelves. It was a small space, as if it had been carved out of an old pantry as an afterthought, and for both of us to fit inside, we had to stand very close. Clara's body gave off a sweet heat—vanilla and patchouli and cherry cigarillos. She offered me a drink.

"Milk?" I said before I could stop myself.

Her lips curled in a wry smile. It was unbearably sexy. "No milk," she said. "Water, whiskey, or wine." *W* words, I thought. How strange.

"Whiskey."

"Good choice." She reached up and brought down two white handleless mugs and a bottle of bourbon.

By now, the sun was slinking downward in the sky and diffuse light fell through the curtainless window, suffusing the kitchen with an ethereal gilt. The whiskey's deep amber glowed. Clara did not offer ice, and though I would have preferred it, I didn't ask for any.

"Let's go out back," she said.

"Clara," I said.

"Sienna?" She turned to me, and the light coming in the window threw her face into shadow. There was, in her features, something so placid, as if she had never expected anything her entire life, and thus had never been disappointed.

"Sorry, nothing," I said. I wanted to ask about the white, wanted to ask why she'd invited me home, wanted to reach my hand out and grab hers, feel her warm palm and supple fingers.

We went through the dining room and out onto the deck. The yard was a small patch of scrubby grass, and beyond that a line of evergreens bordered the incline up to the highway, where I could see the guardrails and cars as they zoomed by.

"You get used to the noise, after a while," she said, sitting in an Adirondack chair. Painted white, as was the deck. I sat next to her in the other Adirondack.

"Are you tenured?" I asked, and then regretted it. What a weird thing to bring up out of nowhere.

"Tenure track, yeah," she said.

"I didn't ask what you teach," I said.

"Philosophy," she said.

"Oh."

"Not a philosophy person, eh?"

I shook my head. "A little abstract for me. I took one class in college. Practically failed."

She laughed and sipped her whiskey. "It isn't like the real world. That's true."

"Why Northampton?" I asked.

"Why not? When you have debts to pay and no one dependent on you, any new town will do."

"Really?"

"No," she said and lapsed into silence. After a while, she said, "I grew up in this house. And my parents gave it to me when they up and relocated to Phoenix. The position opened up at the college and I thought, Why not? I'd been gone seventeen years. Why not come home?"

"Why haven't we met before?" I asked. Poppy and Dale threw parties at least once a month. Certainly Clara would have been invited.

"I don't go out much. I'm pretty solitary."

"Why'd you come to the party today?"

She stared off into the line of trees bordering the yard. "Hard to say. Needed a change of scenery, I guess. What about you?"

"I always go to Poppy's parties. She's my best friend."

"Do you like them?"

"What? The parties or Dale and Poppy?"

"The parties."

"Mostly," I said. "But they can be—what's the right word? Under-stimulating."

She nodded. The way the setting sunlight fell over her face exaggerated her sharp features. I wondered if it did the same for mine—if my neck appeared skinnier, my ears larger.

"Dale and Poppy seem very happy," Clara said.

"They are. They've got the perfect life."

"You think so?"

As soon as she asked, I knew I wasn't really sure. Poppy certainly pretended to be happy if she wasn't, and I went along with it, never questioning or pushing past the surface. Our friendship no longer plumbed the depths the way it once had, in college, and in that disorienting first year out of it. When she married Dale, Poppy entered a world I no longer belonged to, and though I had no real desire to follow her there, I missed the old her—the one that matched me.

But I'd been alone long enough to harness my often disturbing disorientation within the world. Those moments when the solid earth slipped out from under me and left me kicking in the ether. When I woke at night gasping for breath and wondering where I was. With my dad dead, it happened more and more often.

Even the seasons, those trusty indicators of time's passage, seemed to slip and slide away from me. This afternoon, the sultry warmth of it, the drifting, decaying smell of leaves and whisper of cool evening, something cracked open inside me. Nothing, I knew, was as it appeared. "I honestly don't know," I said, answering Clara's question. I had no idea if Poppy's life was really perfect, and I would never dare ask. "Nothing's perfect, I suppose."

Clara and I watched the sun descend. It had been a long time since I'd sat like that—with everything and nothing to say. As the thick gashes of magenta and orange striped the horizon, Clara became not a stranger, but a promise. Dusk settled around us. Bats swooped for mosquitoes. Cars continued to pass by, en route somewhere else. The noise became pleasant, an afterthought, muted the way sound is when you're submerged in water.

Clara said, "I saw you at the party and I recognized you."

"You recognized me?" I said. "From town?"

"No. I mean I recognized you from life. Like déjà vu, or reincarnation. Something like that."

"That's quite a line." I felt my peacefulness dissolve.

"It isn't. I mean it. You looked lost."

"You're not going to start talking about accepting Jesus as my savior, are you?"

"No saviors. I don't believe in that stuff."

"But you believe in past lives?"

"Sometimes. Right now I do." She reached across the space that divided us and rested her hand on my forearm. I allowed her hand to touch me, allowed the strong pull of human contact.

"I'm sorry," she said. "I'm rusty. It's been a while since I've done this."

"I'm not lost," I said, but it had been a long time since I'd let a woman touch me.

Clara brought her eyes to mine. "You're very beautiful," she said, cupping my chin in her hand.

My entire body reeled, and we stared at one another, hooked by the taut line of connection threading between us. If I kissed her now, it would be acknowledging the half-animal that careened inside me. It would be admitting I liked being pulled in by her. And though I wanted it, it seemed too dangerous to let the wild thing loose, desperate as it was for air. What good was a fish with legs? Or a girl with gills?

Clara's lips, her face, were so close. I could smell the whiskey on her breath, the warmth of it mixed with the exhaust in the air and her vanilla perfume. It was an inch, two, to taste her.

A horn blared past, smearing the angry sound across the yard. In a flash I stood, moving through the screen door, to the kitchen, my car. As I put my cup into the sink, the door opened again and Clara was there. "I'm sorry. I didn't mean to upset you."

"You didn't," I said. "But I should go. I—" My words came tumbling out, confused, my mouth cottony from the whiskey, my body flushed. "Why is everything white?"

"I like an empty canvas," she said.

"You're a painter too?"

"No. Metaphorically."

"You don't have anything on the walls."

"It's more about possibility," she said, leaning toward the wall closest to her and drawing something—a name, a curvy mermaid, a violin; I couldn't tell—on it with her finger.

"Isn't that tiresome? Always waiting for what could be?"

"You tell me."

It was as if she'd seen directly into my heart, into all that I'd held close, the protected hopes that I'd been too frightened to fulfill. I walked through life veiling that fragile space, and now someone I barely knew had looked right at it. My life was stalled out. I wanted all those next steps into adulthood I'd not taken: a partner, a house, a family, a career—and at the same time, those steps were a litany of normalcy that I knew would never fit.

We stood staring at one another for what seemed like a long time. My lips were dry, my underarms damp with sweat.

"Sienna." Clara stepped toward me, brought her hand to my

hip. "I meant what I said. You're very beautiful." Her face was so open, so tender.

"Thank you. Thanks for the drink," I said. "But I have to go." I stepped back from her.

"Thanks for letting me drive—it's a great car. Runs like a dream. You must take good care of it."

"It was my father's," I said. My father had taken good care of it.

Clara smiled, slow and sad, and again the wild oxygen of desire flared through me. I let myself out.

I didn't check my phone for messages until I got home. Poppy had texted twice and called once. *Sienna, just wanted to make sure you're okay. You seemed a little out of it and then you disappeared. Call me.*

Most of the night I lay awake, thinking about Clara's narrow nose, her funny poof of hair, the way she'd held my chin so gently in her fingers. When I finally fell asleep, I dreamed of her driving, my hand on her thigh as the streets and houses and trees flew by. I dreamed of a cardinal nesting in a tree choked by bittersweet. I dreamed of breathing underwater.

In the morning, after I'd showered and had coffee, I called Poppy. I had not shaken the steep yearning that filled me, or the strangeness of my dreams. As the phone rang, I looked down and saw I was still wearing the rubies. I twisted the band around and around.

Poppy answered. "You sly devil."

"What?" I asked, though I knew full well.

"You went home with Clara. I knew it. I knew you'd love her."

"Nothing happened."

"Oh, Sienna," she said. "Stop being silly. She called Dale an hour ago and asked for your phone number."

"He gave it to her?" It was as if a wave crashed over me. Poppy sighed. "Of course he did."

"But—"

"But nothing," Poppy said. "You're ready for this."

The gills flared.

Poppy continued, "Clara really, really liked you."

As I had her. I'd found the current. I stopped resisting and followed it upstream.

AN ADVENTURE

Shisuma

My friends think I'm boring. I have a normal job. I drive a Toyota. I like to read, take long romantic walks on the beach, and have nice quiet evenings with a glass of wine and good, interesting company. Oh, and I'm happily married. That about kills them. Because how does anyone in their right mind want to wake up with the same woman day after day? Let alone after ten years. And sex? What a drag. It probably becomes a second job after any extended period of time, until you inevitably quit it altogether. Because let's face it, there's nothing exciting about having the same woman, night after night. But it probably does suit me, because I never was a partygoer and I never really did have that many women. So every time the subject comes up, my friends come to the conclusion that this boring and terribly married life is perfect for me. I always smile and sip my wine, not even trying to defend myself because I know the truth and they wouldn't understand it.

I'm an adventurer, you see. When I come home at night to

the goddess I call my wife and kiss her hello, I know by the fire
in her eyes that burns through my clothes and the way she holds
me just a little longer than necessary that I'm going on a journey
tonight. I love to travel and to discover the desolate places where
only few have gone before me. But there are those places, the
secret places that only I have charted. That's my favorite tour,
because I discover something new every time.

I start at her hair. A waterfall of the deepest red I have ever
seen cascading down her shoulders and whispering on the sheets.
It's a breathtaking sight, like liquid fire. I always lose myself in
the rich scent and the way my fingers disappear when I comb
through the silken strands. But her impatient sighs call me back.
I must resume my journey. The path is familiar as I follow her
brows with my tongue, down the bridge of her nose, taking a
detour to worship at her temples. She giggles when I tease the
rim of her earlobe, but it turns into a moan when I begin to
suck. She urges me on, but I just smile. Tonight won't be a quick
trip. Instead I rest my mouth on her soft lips and discover that
I'm thirsty. She opens up to me, like Ali Baba's cave, revealing
to me all the pleasures that lie inside. My love is thirsty too.
She drinks me in as I explore every inch and dance my tongue
around hers. I always dread my departure from this place of
wonders, but eventually we both have to surface for air. Before
she can protest, I continue, feathering light kisses along my path
down her throat. The road is steep, but I know where it will take
me. She knows it too and pants in anticipation. I surprise her by
stopping at her shoulders first, nibbling the tender flesh at the
base of her neck and tracing my way down her collarbone with
my tongue. Her moans tell me I'm on the right track.

My heart swells when I see it, the valley. It just takes my
breath away. As I dip a finger between her breasts and trace the
contours, I can tell it takes away hers too. But this isn't where I

want to stay, so I hurry uphill over the unbelievable softness of her breasts.

This is heaven. She clearly agrees as she calls God, Jesus, and every other deity known to mankind while I scout her cream-skinned mounds, teasing their peaks but never lingering. This is the hardest part, teasing her until she begs for my mouth on her nipples because I want it just as bad as she does. I ache to devour her. To take her breast in my mouth like a ripe fruit and make her scream. It is one of those moments I live for. But I also like to tease. When we both reach the point that we can't take it any longer I finally close my lips around her nipples. Sucking, biting, worshipping each in turn. Her body bucks and she twines her fingers in my hair, forcing me harder against her while guiding my free hand lower. It doesn't work, though. I planned this trip, so I lead. I keep my hand on the flat planes of her belly and caress little earthquakes to the surface. Making her whimper. My mouth follows eagerly. I'm almost there.

But first the vast, white expanse of her stomach. Kissing, caressing, breathing, making the muscles under me clench and her breathing grow hard and ragged. I tumble in her belly button but come back up fast when I hear her whispered plea. Truth be told, I long for it too. I know what treasure awaits me and I need it. So I hurry through a forest of red that tickles my face to the most precious place on earth, my fountain of youth.

I hold still for a moment, breathing in the scent and savoring the view. She's overflowing. Her need is just as great as mine so I drink, sucking my way through her folds, searching. My lover arches her back and presses against my face, trying to guide me to her last treasure. Her pearl of need. I can't help but smile. She's magnificent, and although I want to stay here and keep her like this forever, I know I can't. So I plunge my fingers into her, filling her, while taking her clit between my lips, sucking hard.

She shouts my victory, her muscles clenching around my fingers. I have never seen a more beautiful sight and it breaks my heart every time. My goddess, my adventure, my fountain of youth. So strong and fierce, so full of life but so vulnerable. She is the only one that takes me to these places and shows me things no one else has ever seen.

My fingers stay inside her, not ready to leave yet, while the rest of me travels back up. I kiss her, long and slow, celebrating my return. She holds my face in her hands, tenderly tracing the contours, telling me she loves me as I slip out of her. I sigh with content and wonder how anyone could find this boring.

Strands of liquid fire dance across my breasts as she straddles me with a dangerous glint in her eyes.

I grin. Oh no, my life isn't boring.

SOFT HANDS AND HARD HATS

JL Merrow

"Bloody hell, it's big!" I turned around slowly, the cavern getting bigger—or seeming like it, at any rate—the more my eyes adjusted to the darkness.

"Big enough to fit York Minster in," a soft voice said from behind me.

I turned and saw a girl my height, wearing a hard hat. Well, we were all wearing hard hats. Health and Safety, and all that bollocks. But hers wasn't a battered old one, borrowed from the Craven Pothole Club, its original color obliterated by a layer of dried-on mud. Her hat was bright yellow, only slightly muddy, and it fitted her well. Her hard hat *suited* her.

"Be a bit of a bugger getting it down the shaft, though," I said.

She smiled, her teeth catching a glimmer of light that filtered down from the entrance, hundreds of feet above us. "Maybe they could take it down in pieces and build it again from in here like a big Lego set. I'm Kim, by the way. I'm a Craven Caver."

"Han," I said. "Short for Hannah. I'm an aging raver."

She burst out laughing, a rich sound that filled that huge cave easily. "I don't believe that for a minute! You don't look a day over twenty-five."

I'm thirty. Oops—clean slipped my mind to tell her, though. Funny, that. "In this light, I could be a hundred and twenty-five and you'd be none the wiser."

"Maybe, but you'd be amazed how many centenarians we don't get coming down here."

"You're not marketing it right. Tell 'em it's half-price on Tuesdays, and you'll be snowed under with grannies. Course, they'll all be wanting cups of tea and bourbon biscuits."

"We could set up a café in the main chamber, perhaps," she mused, cocking her head to one side. "The Gaping Gill Gourmet."

"Or the Pothole Parlor. You're not from round here, are you?" I nearly bit my tongue off after I'd said it, in case she'd think I was making a dig about the color of her skin. In the shadows, it was ebony, but when the light hit her face I could see warmer tones shine through.

Me all over, that. Opening my mouth and bunging my size sevens straight in. Not even pausing to wipe them first.

Her smile didn't waver for a second, though, and I breathed again. "No, I'm a soft Southern Jessie from Hampshire," she said.

"You don't look that soft to me," I said, lying through my teeth. She was all curves, hips swelling below a trim little waist cinched in with a utility belt, and her breasts firm and neat above. She looked soft as velvet. No iron beneath, neither. Least, I didn't think so. And her voice was satin cushions on a four-poster bed. "I went down to Hampshire once. We had a holiday in the New Forest. Camping, we were. Couldn't move for bloody ponies."

She laughed again. "Most people like ponies, you know."

"That's because most people don't have them sticking their noses in the tent at four o'clock in the morning. Or leaving bloody big piles of you-know-what right where they're about to put their bare feet."

"Okay, I can understand why they might not be your favorite animals after that." She chewed on her bottom lip for a moment. "Are you here on your own?"

I opened my mouth to answer, but then Nicole came barging in and answered for me. "It's grand here, isn't it? Are we going off exploring?" She clapped an arm around my shoulder.

Flummoxed, I gazed around at the huge open space. Folk were milling around, and another bod was coming down on the chair. "Can see it all from here, can't we? Niccie, this is—"

"Oh, there's more than this. I was talking to this bloke over there, and he said there's all kinds of passages off to the sides. Said it's the best bit. You don't want to miss that, do you?"

"What do you think, Kim?" I asked desperately. I could see she was about to wander off and find some other bugger to talk to.

"I could show you and your friend around, if you like," she said, her gaze flickering between us.

Nicole finally noticed I'd been talking to someone. "Oh, right—are you one of the cavers, then?"

"This is Kim, and yeah, she's a Craven Caver." I couldn't say it without smiling. "Kim, this is my mate Niccie." I hoped she noticed the stress I'd put on the word *mate*. Niccie had, from the look she sent me, so I guessed she'd be ripping the shit out of me later about it all.

"Okay, then," Kim said, her smile brighter than the lamp on her helmet. "Let's go caving!"

Right then, I reckon if she'd said, "Know what? There's this bloody big cliff here, do you want to jump off?" I'd have acted just the same. I nodded enthusiastically, and my hard hat fell down over my eyes. "Bugger. Yeah, all right."

"Great!" I was right about her being soft. Gentle fingers came up to my throat and tightened the strap of my hat.

I just hoped she wouldn't think it strange I didn't take a breath the whole time she was touching me.

Least, not until Niccie prodded me and I gasped in air with a noise like a punctured whale.

"All set now?" Kim asked. "It's this way. The passages get a bit narrow, but you'll be fine getting through."

I nodded, and nothing happened this time, so I followed Kim and Niccie into this sort of crack in the wall of the cave. I couldn't work out whether to go forward and let my hips scrape on the sides, or sideways, which meant my boobs got in the way. I ended up twisting awkwardly, all of me at different angles.

"We're caving, not doing the sand dance," Niccie said, laughing at me.

"Hey, we're not all stick insects like you," I muttered back.

We could walk upright at first, but then the tunnel got lower and we had to bend down. It killed your back after a while. A bit farther on we were crawling—knackered my knees, but it was right muddy and all, so that padded it a bit. After a bit of that, it got even tighter, and then we had to inch along on our bellies like a load of bloody earthworms, and guess what?

It was right then I found out I was claustrophobic.

I could feel the weight of all those rocks pressing down on me, like they were squeezing the air right out of my lungs. I tried to remember—was it better to take deep breaths or quick shallow ones? Because one of those made you hyperventilate and I wasn't sure which, and what were the chances of anyone having a paper bag for me to breathe into down here? There was no room to turn round and I couldn't face trying to wriggle backward—what if I got wedged in and couldn't go backward or forward? Niccie and Kim wouldn't be able to get out, for that matter, and they'd either have to wait till I got thinner like Winnie-the-Pooh or else chop bits off me with penknives like that poor bloke in Utah they made the film about.

So I had to keep on going and try to breathe, somehow.

Just as I was thinking I couldn't take it any longer, we came out into this big cave—well, not that big, about the size of my mum's front room, I suppose, but bloody hell, it was better than that tunnel. I tried to slow my breathing down to normal without anyone noticing, but my heart was beating so loud I wondered why it didn't echo off the cave walls.

We shone our torches around, seeing uneven walls, a floor with boulders big enough to sit on, and stalactites hanging down from the ceiling. Their stalagmites reached up, desperate to touch them. There were some lads already in there, and they were just about to go on farther through the passages.

Kim said hi to them and told them to stick together and make sure they didn't get lost. And then she turned back to us and said, "Right—ready to go farther?"

"Too right!" Niccie said. "It's like *Lord of the Rings* down here." Then she made her eyes all big. "Where'sssss the preciousssss?"

"Is it in its pocketsessssss?" one of the lads asked, with an admiring look over my mate's figure.

"Wanna come here and check?" she teased back. She's an equal-opportunity flirt, Niccie is. Always has been.

"Oi, get a room, you two," I muttered. "Or a cave, or something."

She gave me a look and a fake cough that sounded a lot like "pot." Fair dues, I was standing a bit close to Kim at the time. There was a boulder on the other side crowding me. Honest.

"Okay," Kim said. "Let's go, then."

Bugger. Moment of truth. "I don't think I can," I blurted out. "Sorry. Turns out I'm a bit claustrophobic." I thought it sounded better, putting it that way, than "wild horses with their tails on fire couldn't drag me another inch through these caves."

Kim looked at me, concerned, which made my breathing go funny all over again. "Do you want to head back to the main chamber?"

My mouth went dry at the thought of going through that narrow, crushing passageway again so soon. "Um, in a bit," I squeaked.

"Okay, how about I stay here with you while the others go on? And when they come back, we can all go back together?"

"You can't do that," I said. "You're a potholer, not a baby-sitter. You go on, I'll be fine." Lying through my teeth again. But I didn't fancy admitting to Kim that I was too much of a big girl's blouse to stay here by myself.

"Oh, I've been all over these caves. I don't need to do it again. Be glad to put my feet up for a bit, actually." She smiled and sat down on a boulder. "Come on, pull up a rock."

"You going to be all right?" Niccie's lad asked. I think he wanted to look caring and sensitive.

"She'll be fine," Niccie said impatiently. She's never been that big on caring and sensitive. Then again, she probably had a fair idea I wouldn't mind being left alone with Kim for a while.

"Go on, stop cluttering the place up," I told them. "There's hardly room to swing a cat with you lot in here."

"Well, if you're sure you don't want to come...." She grinned, the shadows painting her face with wicked insinuation.

Or maybe it was there already.

"Bugger off, the lot of you," I said, and finally, they did.

I sat down next to Kim, feeling awkward now we were alone.

Our hips pressed together; bit narrow, that rock was. Honest.

"Don't feel bad about it," she said, and for a moment I thought she was talking about me sitting so close to her. "Oh—the claustrophobia," I realized, and felt like a muppet. "It's never hit me like that before—I mean, I've never liked being closed in, but I've never felt like I couldn't breathe before." I sighed. "You must think I'm a right wuss."

"It's heights, for me," she said, her voice soothing my ears. "I get all dizzy and have to close my eyes."

I stared at her. "But—what about the chairlift?"

"I've been up and down on it dozens of times, and I still hate it. But it's worth it, to get down here. I just love it, underground. Have you ever seen true dark? Not like this," she said, waving her hand at the shadows that danced on the walls of the cave with the motion of her head. "I mean, no light at all. Not the sort of dark you get in cities, where there's always streetlights and house lights—or even in the countryside, because on clear nights you get the stars, and on cloudy nights you get the reflection of lights from miles away. I'm talking real blackness, the sort you can touch, you can taste. You only get that underground."

"No," I whispered. "I've never seen that."

"Would you like to?"

My heart was back in my mouth, but all I said was, "All right."

I flicked off my torch, and she dimmed her headlamp—then turned it off altogether.

The darkness was like a thick blanket wrapped around my head. It was terrifying. It brought it home to me, how far down we were and how small we were. How easily we could be crushed by all those tons of rock over our heads. But at the same time, we could have been anywhere. All alone, just us two. I could hear Kim breathing beside me, feel the warmth of her cross the space between us.

"It's amazing, isn't it?" she whispered.

"Scary," I whispered back. Funny how it's easier to be honest in the dark. I felt a cool, dry hand slip into mine, and the tingling spread from my fingers right up my arm to my heart. "Don't put the lights back on yet, though," I said quickly. I wasn't scared; not when I was touching her.

I swear I heard her smile, just a catch in her breathing. "I won't. So what do you do, Han, when you're not getting claustrophobic down potholes?"

"Me?" I tried to think of something that sounded exciting. Came up blank. "I'm an ecologist. Work for Yorkshire Wildlife Trust, near Doncaster."

"Sounds great—you must really make a difference, doing what you do. I'm just a bank clerk in Barnsley," she said, like it was something to be ashamed of.

Bugger that. "You're not *just* anything," I said, squeezing her hand. She squeezed back, so I surged on before I could let my nerves get the better of me. "Are you seeing anyone?"

"What, in this dark?" Kim laughed. "No," she said, her voice flowing over me like honey. "I'm not seeing anyone. I had a girlfriend back in Portsmouth, but, well... Long-distance relationships aren't easy, are they?"

I hugged the darkness to me, breathing in its sudden warmth. "Barnsley's pretty close to Doncaster. Only about twenty miles, I'd say."

"Less, I think," Kim whispered. "Maybe we should measure it some time. Together." She raised my hand to her unseen lips. Her kiss wasn't cold, but it still sent shivers right through me. I slid my arm around her waist, and we shared our warmth under our thick black blanket. I turned my face to kiss her, and we giggled as our hard hats knocked together. "Shall we try that again?" I whispered. "You go left, I'll go right. No, hang about, that's not right. How about we both go left—our left? That ought to do it."

This time, our lips met. Hers were full and warm, and they welcomed me in. She tasted of tea and cool places and Kendal Mint Cake, and there was nothing in the world I wouldn't have braved for her kiss. I closed my eyes as I kissed her and behind my eyelids it wasn't dark anymore. I could see her, clear as day, her beautiful brown eyes dancing with fun.

"Do this a lot down potholes, do you?" I asked, breathless and dizzy, when we broke apart.

She laughed. "Not a lot, no. Never met anyone down a pothole I wanted to kiss before."

We held each other in the dark, and kissed some more and talked about stuff, like you do. Well, whispered, really. It didn't feel right, being loud in that pitch-black quietness, broken only by odd sounds coming down the tunnels and the drip-drip-drip of water.

It was the voices that told us when the others came back. One of the lads spoke and Niccie cackled with laughter. Then light from their torches trickled unevenly into the cave, washing away our safe blanket of darkness. Kim and I let go of each other. What we had was private, not for Niccie and the lads to snigger over.

"Han? You in there?" Niccie called, her voice echoey in the passages, and Kim squeezed my hand, then let it go. It felt cold without her.

"Yeah, we're here," I called, as Kim switched her headlamp back on.

I blinked at its brightness as Niccie and the lads burst back into our cavern. It was smaller than I'd pictured it as we sat there in the dark. Funny how your mind plays tricks on you. It'd felt larger than the main cavern, with just the two of us in it, and all of it had been ours. Now it was back to being barely the size of my mum's front room.

"Been having fun, have you?" Niccie asked with a knowing grin.

"Nah," I said straight-faced. "Bit boring, really, waiting for you lot to finish gallivanting around the underworld." But I couldn't help glancing over at Kim and smiling.

"Yeah, you know what?" Niccie said, with sarcasm that could bite clean through a stalagmite. "As soon as I saw you, I thought, there's a girl who looks really bored."

"Are you ready to go back now?" Kim asked me, and I nodded, hoping I looked more certain than I felt. "Just remember—it'll get wider all the time, this way. So you'll always know the worst is behind you."

"You go in front," I told her. "Then I'll have to keep going, right?"

We let Niccie and the lads lead the way, then Kim followed. As she bent to creep into the passageway, she turned. "You're sure about this? Sure you don't want to go first?"

"No," I said. "I'll follow you." *Anywhere*, I could have added, but Niccie might just have heard and she'd never have let me live it down.

I almost seized up when I had to get into that tiny crack between the rocks, down on my belly like a snake, but not half as agile. My breathing started to go, but I flicked on my torch and shone it on Kim's boot soles, moving ahead of me at a slug's pace, and I thought about how grand it'd be to take those off her and play with the toes within. Before I knew it I'd slithered in behind her. I just kept my mind on those feet. I wondered if she painted her toenails, and if she wore rings on her toes like in the nursery rhyme. Did she like to wear heels when she went out for the night? And all the time, somehow, I managed to keep breathing, keep moving.

"Okay there, Han?" she asked from time to time, and I answered with a "Yeah" or a "Fine" and I knew she wouldn't take offense. There'd be time for proper talking when we were out of here.

Some lovely bugger had been at that passageway while we were in the cave, and they'd shortened it, I reckoned. Wasn't that long before we were off our knees and crouching. Kim reached a hand back to me and I squeezed it tight, then let it go again. Hard enough walking through here without trying to hang on to someone as well. My thigh muscles ached and my back didn't like it much either, but then the passage opened out again and I could see light past the bodies in front.

We sidled out into the main chamber, which seemed even bigger than I'd remembered. Looking up to the roof, a hundred and fifty feet above us, I took a deep breath of chill air. It tasted sweet, but no sweeter than my Kim's lips.

"You did it!" she said softly, and I saw the gleam of her smile.

As we neared the bottom of the chairlift, the lights got brighter.

"Bloody hell, Han, we're all covered in t' mud!" Niccie cackled. Her lad had his arm around her. I supposed I'd better think about finding out his name. She was right, too—head-to-toe mudlarks, the lot of us.

Kim had a smear of dried mud on her cheek, pale against her skin. She smiled at me. "You've got mud on your nose," she said. "Want me to get it for you?"

"Is it worth it?" I asked, looking down at myself ruefully. Thank god I'd worn full waterproofs. Even if they did make me look like a walking tent. Now I looked like a tent after a weekend at Glastonbury.

"Probably not. Still, nothing a hot shower won't cure."

I felt a bit hot myself, her voice conjuring pictures in my brain. "We're staying at a B-and-B back at Horton in Ribblesdale, me and Niccie. Don't suppose you'd like to come back with us?"

Kim's face twisted. "Can't—I'll have to stay and help dismantle the winch, it's our last day here. By the time we've done that—well, and had a few drinks—I won't be fit for anything but sleep. But we'll swap numbers up top, all right?"

"All right," I said.

We watched a lad being strapped into the chairlift, flirting with the caver doing the strapping.

"Okay," the girl said as she finished the last buckle and stepped back. "When you get up to the top, you give us a yodel, all right?"

He grinned. "Got it."

"It's traditional, but I'm always too scared," Kim whispered. We watched as he rose up and up, the ceiling of the cave seeming to get higher as he did, until he started to block the sunlight coming down that big chimney. Then he let out a great call, whooping like one of the monkeys in Chester Zoo, and disappeared.

"You'll be fine," I told Kim.

"I know, I know—I'm just being daft, really."

"No dafter than me thinking a cave that's stood for a million bloody years is going to pick today to fall in on me."

"Actually, it's more like eleven or twelve thousand years old. Since the last ice age."

I laughed. "Good thing you didn't tell me that back there, then."

"You were so brave," Kim said, her hand slipping into mine. "I was worried you'd freeze up or hyperventilate, but you just kept on going."

"Had an incentive, didn't I?" I squeezed her hand. "Didn't want you getting away from me."

"Oh, don't you worry," she teased back. "Climbers and cavers are known for keeping a firm grip on things."

We watched Niccie and the lads going up on the chair. The lads all howled like werewolves when they got to the top, and Niccie screeched out a battle cry I thought would bring down the whole bloody cavern.

Then it was our turn. I made Kim go first, and I saw how her fingers were trembling as she held onto the harness. "You'll be fine," I told her, and she managed a smile.

I watched her soar up toward the daylight, and my heart ached to think of her scared, with her eyes tight shut. I'd loved the trip on the way down, being gently sprayed by the thin summer flow of the waterfall and passing sheer rock walls with brave flowers and plants clinging stubbornly to life. I wished I could be up there with Kim now, holding her close so she wouldn't be frightened.

Then I heard her voice, yodeling down from the top of the cavern. "Woo-hoooooooo!"

My heart soared up to join her, and I couldn't wait for the rest of me to follow.

LAW OF THE CAMAZOTZ

Lisa Figueroa

The moment I stepped off the plane in Cancun, the heat surrounded me like a feverish demon, both sticky and slick, attacking in shimmering waves of unrelenting sweat. It seemed to cling to me, particularly focusing its wet mouth—if such a thing even had a mouth, which I'm pretty sure it would—directly on my pussy as my knees threatened to collapse from the sheer force of its intensity. I knew it would be hot in the middle of August, I knew the humidity in the southernmost part of Mexico would very likely be uncomfortable, but this was almost inhuman. What had I been thinking, agreeing to a vacation in such tropical weather? With a sigh of dismay I noted that my long, curly hair was morphing into a mass of unmanageable frizz. I shot a disapproving look at my sister, Marga, who stood next to me with our luggage, grinning back at me like she'd just unwrapped this paradise on Christmas morning. When we were kids, she was the one who had always managed to wake up first, desperate to see the toys Santa left her, and then she'd drag me sleepily out of bed to follow her to the Christmas tree. She was always in a hurry, rampaging through her gifts like someone might cancel the holiday any minute, while I preferred to take my time and savor each wrapped bundle. I even tried to guess what was inside. It drove her nuts and she'd eventually abandon her opened boxes and wander over and sit in front of me on folded legs, tilted head resting on her hand as she stared at my efforts like she was trying to figure out how we could ever be related.

We were the same way when it came to our love life. Despite the fact that I was attracted to women and she to men, she tore through her men, eagerly unwrapping them as soon as possible and then discarding them just as quickly when what she found inside wasn't to her liking. I, on the other hand, was content to explore each of my women slowly, always looking to discover something new inside each one, never wanting to give up even when I knew better.

"God, Antonia, I love the heat. It makes me feel so fucking alive. I think I never want to leave," my sister announced with a throaty and cheerful inflection I hadn't heard in a while, at least not since her breakup with Marco.

I suppose that was the point of this vacation. To get to a happy place, to commiserate together as only sisters can and in the process help each other get over our exes. If only I could laugh about Delia. I was particularly bitter about my breakup with her because she had cheated on me. It had devastated me because I never saw it coming. I was too busy thinking of future dreams, of us moving in together, instead of the reality of her betrayal. I pushed away the memory as I regarded my sister with a wan smile of resignation.

"Great. You feel alive and I feel like I'm dying. I can see this is going to be a wonderful trip."

"Just give it a chance, will you? Don't start checking out on me yet. Let's at least check *in* to the hotel first, *hermana*."

I nodded compliance and headed toward the hotel, very intrigued by the idea of getting inside and basking in the comfort of air-conditioning.

The hotel room was nicer than I'd imagined, terra-cotta floor tiles, handcrafted rustic furniture mixed with modern paintings and luxurious bed linens. Authentic but comfortable. I went immediately toward the wall panel to flip on the air conditioner as Marga opened the French doors that led out onto a small balcony, and with a quick smile over her shoulder at me, she went outside. I flopped onto the bed, only slightly feigning exhaustion. When I realized that Marga had no intention of coming back into the coolness of the room, I got up to join her on the balcony. She was leaning with her elbows on the rim of the wrought-iron enclosure, watching the breaking waves and cascading foam. It was a lovely view and took the edge off the unrelenting heat.

"So, what should we do first, grab lunch or go on that diving tour of the caves?" Marga asked without taking her gaze off the ocean.

Marga was an experienced diver. She'd been talking about diving in the wondrous stalagmite caves of the famed Dos Ojos caverns for days. She had several brochures that showed beautiful pure and tranquil water and unique rock formations that turned the caves into another world. There was so much to see that even the bats that lived and roosted high up among the stalactites didn't bother her as much as I thought they would. But I was not in the mood for adventure. Anyway, it wasn't like we were a married couple. We were each free to do as we pleased.

"How about you go diving and I'll go shopping," I said lightly. She blinked in surprise, not sure if she was supposed to be happy about my suggestion or act disappointed.

"Well, okay, but we'll meet back at the hotel for dinner? How's that sound?" she said with a little too much enthusiasm. *So much for acting disappointed.* *"Perfecto,"* I replied. I left her to her personal commune with the natural wonders of Mexico as I grabbed my bag and went to commune with the simple splendor I often found shopping.

On the advice of the front desk, I walked six blocks away from the beach and turned left onto the main street of the town. It supposedly offered the best variety of shopping. There were several shops that sold the usual tourist trinkets; sandal key chains, T-shirts and wide brimmed hats, but a few stood out with lovely and authentic Mexican crafts: leather bags with incredible tooled design, delicately painted Talavera pottery, hand-woven blankets with intricate detail and Alebrijes, papier-mâché sculptures in the shape of every known animal.

By the time I reached the end of several blocks, and the limit of how many shopping bags I could comfortably carry, I decided to take a break. I stopped at a café for a soda, sipping it as I stretched my tired legs and rubbed my sore arms, people-watching while luxuriating in the cooling air. It was then I noticed how much darker the day was getting. Twilight was settling in and I decided it was time to head back to the hotel. Actually, if I didn't hurry, I was going to miss my dinner date with Marga.

The light faded even faster as I made my way down the winding streets. I kept looking at the shops around me for help in distinguishing landmarks, but I couldn't seem to note anything familiar, and when I turned the next corner, I realized with a fluster of anxiety that I was lost. I was about to take out my cell phone when a man walked up to me out of nowhere.

"Hola, señorita. Can I interest you in some silver? I have bracelets, rings, necklaces. What would you like?" He opened

up his coat and I found myself gazing at an amazing display of jewelry arranged neatly on the inside lining. "*No, gracias,*" I said, moving around him. He quickly moved back in front of me. I hesitated before firmly stepping past him again but he blocked my way and stared at me without smiling. "Can't you see she's not interested, Gonzalo?" Another larger man came up behind me and I felt momentary relief that someone had come to offer help. That relief vanished quickly as he clamped his hand over my mouth and together they pulled me into a darkened alley. I screamed but it was muffled, and I lost my bags as I tried to pull away and kicked out, making contact with the smaller one's knee as they increased their speed. I wasn't sure if I tripped or was pushed, but the ground rushed up at me and I banged the side of my forehead hard. The larger man released my mouth to roll me over, and as he did so I was finally free to scream my lungs out. Although the first, smaller guy was startled into letting me go, the other pulled back his hand, quickly closing it into a fist as I closed my eyes in sick anticipation, but the blow never reached me. Instead, the resounding thud I heard was the large man being hauled against the side of the building before he crumpled at my feet. The smaller man slinked away, his jewelry coat jingling as he turned and ran. He didn't get very far, and in a flurry of movement too quick to understand, he was soon unconscious on the ground next to his friend.

I closed my eyes in relief but I was also stunned and confused as to what had just happened. When I finally opened them again, someone was crouching next to me. A woman with eyes that reminded me of the dark turquoise diving pools my sister was probably exploring somewhere in those caverns deep beneath us. Long, silky black hair was gathered loosely in a clip at the nape of her neck, and her bronzed skin had a burnished quality like smooth terra-cotta sculpture. Her clothes were dark and indistinguishable except for a long leather coat that for some reason reminded me of a superhero cape.

I tried sitting up but the motion made me want to vomit, so I lay back down and blinked as she bent closer, assessing my injuries. "You're going to be okay," the woman said as she touched my face briefly, almost longingly. She withdrew her hand and smiled.

"Who are you?" I asked.

"My name's Caliana. And you are?"

"Antonia."

Even though she nodded, I wasn't sure if she'd heard me. She was paying particularly close attention to my bleeding temple. I had a hard time focusing because my vision wouldn't stop whiting out and her eyes kept transforming into six dancing pairs of blue. The last thing I remember was her leaning forward to cradle the back of my head with her palm, hot breath panting across my forehead as she soothingly traced her tongue across my bleeding wound with purposeful flicks.

I woke up slowly as the sounds of crashing waves and salty, moist air invaded my senses. For a moment, before I opened my eyes, I imagined I was floating out in the middle of the sea, drifting, guided only by the fickle whimsies of the wind. The feeling of letting go was peaceful and I didn't want it to end, but I knew it was time to come ashore, and since I was curious to see where I landed, I opened my eyes. I was lying in a soft bundle of blankets on some kind of raised dais. A bamboo table and matching chairs were on one side of me and a small sink and stove on the other. My shopping bags were neatly arranged against the wall. The illumination of several candles gave off an eerie glow that made shadows appear and disappear. I sat up reluctantly, not wanting to leave the comfort of the cocoon-like bed. I remembered my head wound and tentatively touched it but there was no trace of the previous cut; no pain either, even when I rubbed my forehead harder. No anything. It was as if it had never existed. *But it did happen, didn't it?*

"Hello?" I called out, unsure of anything, and my echoing voice seemed to taunt me. I realized I was in a cave.

"Hello," my rescuer, Caliana, answered in the same instant I felt a rush of air next to me that appeared to morph into her solid form. A wave of dizziness flooded through me as I turned toward her and blinked, trying to focus. She smiled at me shyly. "It's good to see you awake."

"You saved my life," I said.

"Not really. Those guys were just robbing you. They weren't going to kill you. They had you targeted the moment you went to Gato's Café."

I remembered the look on their faces and the promise of brutality in the grip of their hands. Somehow I knew she was downplaying the seriousness of the attack. "But you stopped them. I don't understand how you were able to do that."

"I know some martial arts," she said with a shrug. She gently touched the place on my temple where my cut had been. "How do you feel?"

My eyes widened at the coolness of her touch and the simplicity of her explanation. Her strength was something I'd never seen in anyone, let alone a woman. She'd handled those men like she was twice their size. I wondered why that didn't scare me more as I looked around, still trying to get my bearings. It was night now but her olive skin glowed as if lit by more than simple candles, and her eyes sparkled as if there was something hovering just beneath the surface of those tranquil turquoise pools, something that kept wavering as she regarded me with a deepening intensity. I wanted to sink back into the cocoon bed. *With her.* That last thought made me light-headed again. "Thank you."

It was all I could manage to say.

She tilted her head as if she'd never heard these words before, her lips pressed together in a slight frown, and then she brightened again. "If you really want to thank me, then stay and have dinner with me. I just caught some excellent fish."

Had she also caught me? "You mean you not only know martial arts but you can cook too?" I smiled mischievously at her and she chuckled.

"I can do a lot of things that might surprise you."

I quivered with an overwhelming wish to know what those *things* might be.

"I'd love to have dinner with you," I said.

"Good," she replied and stood up as she offered a hand to me.

I clasped her hand, and as I got up from the bed and stepped down off its platform, I stumbled and fell clumsily into her arms. She caught me instantly, our faces inches from each other, breathing each other's breath, the warm softness of my full breasts pressed up hard against her smaller, flatter chest. As I felt her nipples contract through her thin shirt, my arms tightened around her shoulders and her hands gripped my waist. A soft moan escaped her just before she released me and stepped away.

"Careful. You might need to take it a bit easy for a while," she said without looking at me.

"Is there somewhere I could freshen up a little?" I asked.

"In the back, to your right, there's an alcove that will have anything you need."

She had already grabbed a small basket from the table and was busying herself with the preparations for dinner. I found my way to the alcove and made a quick phone call to Marga, who was upset that I was not meeting her for dinner.

"I can't believe you already have a hot date," Marga said with a tinge of jealously.

"Well, I don't know if I'd call being in a cave with a stranger a hot date."

"You're in a cave?" There was panicky edge to her voice. "My diving guide said the caves have an unusual number of bats this season. God, they were everywhere."

"That's strange. I haven't seen any."

"Just be careful. Anyway, I guess I get to have a boring evening with room service. I don't feel comfortable going out by myself."

I said good-bye, amused that for once I was the one willing to get out there and take a chance and my sister was afraid to even go down to the bar and have a drink by herself. It was actually satisfying to see our roles reversed. My attack had left me feeling a little reckless, along with a definite sense of exasperation at my sister's fear and hesitation. I supposed I finally understood the way Marga usually saw me. When I got back to the main room, Caliana was setting the table. She looked up at me, and her appreciative glance made me shiver even though I wasn't the least bit cold.

Dinner was a heady blur of shy glances and longing looks. My host was incredibly attractive. She was androgynously gorgeous in a way that surprised me, since I usually went for femmes like me, but her slim hips and boyish body were a nice counterpoint to my generous curves. I could tell by the way she kept staring at my cleavage that the attraction was mutual. There was a soothing calmness about her, a sort of sensuous ease that made me comfortable but also made me vibrate with desire. I had never felt such potent attraction. I ate every bit of my exquisitely prepared red snapper and finished off two glasses of wine. When she was about to pour a third glass I shook my head. I noticed Caliana had barely touched her food. It seemed like she was very good at moving the food around her plate. I couldn't help but wonder what Marga would do in this situation. At the moment, I was tired of being careful. The more careful I was, the worse I seemed to do when it came to women. Maybe it was time to be bold.

"So, do you take a lot of women back here to your cave?" I asked.

She looked up sharply at the question. "No. This is actually the first time I've ever brought anyone here. It's the first time I've ever wanted to bring someone."

"I don't do things like this either. I don't usually end up in someone's hideaway."

"I know. That's probably why I brought you here. I couldn't help myself."

She gazed at me with unabashed desire and my heart skipped a beat. I was overwhelmed by my own lust, by the hot ache to lose myself in her and to have her lost in me. *But just who is she, and who am I, that not knowing doesn't seem to matter?*

"I think I should go now." The words blurted out despite my resolve and I stood up, unable to stop myself from falling back on old inhibitions. I was intimidated by her attractiveness and my own inability to withstand it. In a flurry of movement, Caliana was standing before me.

"Are you afraid of me?" There was unmistakable hurt in her eyes. "I would never let anyone harm you. Don't you know how lovely you are? You are worthy of so much more than what you've settled for. Let me show you, Antonia."

I looked away, and with the tip of her forefinger, she guided my chin toward her and my gaze back to her own. She dipped in close and our mouths met in a tentative kiss, her cool lips seeking out the warmth of mine as our tongues met, tangling in a rush of hot, strangely pleasant wetness. I pushed her back toward the bed until we fell into the pile of blankets. She held me tight as I landed on top of her, straddling her and grinding my pussy hard against hers. Her hands were both firm and gentle as she briefly cupped my head, her fingers buried in the silk of my cascading curls, before she explored my body, smoothing down my back and lingering on my curvy hips and ass. I couldn't compete with her strength as she maneuvered me onto my back and began to unbutton my blouse. With a sigh I closed my eyes and tilted my head back. When I opened them, I gazed absently up at the ceiling and noticed subtle movement. I blinked, trying to focus better, but the dim candlelight made it difficult to see much beyond shadows. But then I saw them. Several little eyes staring back at me. Bats. Hundreds, most likely thousands of bats. More bats than I'd ever seen in my life. More bats than I ever wanted to see in my life. I screamed and clutched at Caliana, who froze in confusion. As soon as I screamed, it was as if I'd raised an invisible gauntlet and in one stunningly coordinated action, the bats swooped down all around us, shrieking in a cacophony of fury. I could feel the soft rushing of air, of wings fluttering so close, surrounding us until all the light of the cave vanished. She covered me with her body and whispered, "Shh, they won't hurt you. You've frightened them. They think they might have to protect me."

I frowned. *Are they pets?* She closed her eyes for a brief moment and whispered something I couldn't quite hear, and in another abrupt but precise military-style flight pattern, the bats reversed direction and returned to their prior posts on the ceiling once again, still and quiet as if their chaotic flurry had never happened. Caliana resumed kissing my neck and exposed cleavage, my shirt now open down the front.

"Wait." I wriggled out of her arms and sat up. "Who are you and what are you doing living in a cave full of bats?"

She laughed. "What do you think it means?"

I swallowed a dry mouthful of air and rubbed absently at my invisible head wound. Was it possible I hit my head harder than I thought and was now hallucinating? There was only one other explanation, though completely ridiculous. "Oh, come on. Don't tell me. You're a vampire?"

"Vampire? But that's so unimaginative, *mi amor*. I am a Camazotz."

"Camazotz? What is a Camazotz?" I wasn't really sure I wanted to know the answer.

"In my Mayan culture, it means literally 'death bat.'"

She said this very casually as she took off her shirt and began to unbutton her pants. I didn't know what to say or do. I just gaped at her in disbelief. Right before she took off her pants, she stared back and said with a slow smile, "What are you waiting for? Take off your clothes."

It was as if I no longer had control of my fingers or limbs and had to obey her command. I removed my shorts and sandals, peeled off my already opened blouse and unhooked my bra until I lay back on the blankets completely naked. She examined my body closely, running her icy hand up my thighs, brushing lightly across my pussy and smoothing fingers over my flat stomach. She paid special attention to my breasts, cupping their heavy fullness before squeezing each nipple firmly between her thumb and forefinger as I gasped and squirmed at her touch. Still fondling and pinching my nipples, she dipped her head and kissed me, searching out my tongue in sweet hunger. When she released my lips, I pushed her head down toward my heaving breasts again and watched as she captured one hardened nipple, circling it with her tongue in steady licks until she lightly nipped it with sharp teeth. I cried out at the sudden pain, which disappeared just as suddenly as she began sucking hard, drawing as much of me into her mouth as she could. I grasped the back of her head as I groaned and arched my back, instinctively opening my thighs and bucking my hips. She molded her lean body into mine, spreading my legs even more and rocking her hips between them as she buried her face in the side of my neck. I tensed waiting for pain, waiting for the bite. Wasn't that what she was going to do? *Isn't that what vampires do?* Instead she kissed the velvet skin of my throat and rested her mouth there. When I had been lulled into a false sense of security that she was giving only pleasure and no pain, I felt the abrupt sharp stab of her teeth and warmth of my blood oozing out of the wound. That prior nip had been nothing compared to this, a tantalizing mix of pain and pleasure. Every time I winced in pain, the discomfort was immediately replaced with the exquisite pleasure of her now-scorching tongue and lips.

She smoothed her fingers around the back of my neck with one hand, holding me in place, and with her other, pushed my chin up gently, encouraging me to expose as much of my neck as possible. Which I did eagerly. Eventually, she released her hold on my face and brought her free hand down to my pussy, sliding along the inner folds of my labia, exploring tentatively within the honeyed wetness. She easily slipped her fingers deep within me while using her thumb to massage my clit, and fucked me in synch with her determined sucking. I keened out a high-pitched moan, placing my hand over the four fingers pumping into me furiously. I marveled at her strength and skill, clawing desperately at her back as her fiery mouth clamped even more powerfully onto my neck. The sensations were almost too much, the giving and the taking, how I fed on her purposeful touch the way she fed on my blood, the way it felt so equal but more importantly, felt right, *like we were bringing each other to life.* I shuddered, trying to keep the orgasm at bay for as long as I could before finally giving in, letting go, as the surge of pleasure engulfed me in a blinding rush like droves of swooping bats fluttering, pulsing inside me and around me.

I almost passed out, but when I was able to catch my breath, Caliana was nuzzling and licking the wound on my neck as it throbbed like an overzealous hickey. She gathered me in her arms and I placed my cheek against her heart, relieved to hear it thumping steadily. At least she was real, warmer than before, almost feverish actually, and I had that welcoming feeling of being protected and cocooned again as I rested against her body.

"Since you bit me, does that mean I'm a vampire too?" I asked hesitantly. *Is that what I want?*

She smiled as she caressed my cheek tenderly. "No, *querida,* I've simply marked you as mine. Even if you leave Cancun, you'll come back. You'll have to return to me."

"I don't know if I even want to leave Cancun, let alone come back. I have so many questions."

"I know. We have time enough for them. We have the rest of the night at least. But first, there are other, more important things to attend to." She wrapped her long legs around me and pulled me closer and I lost any further rational thought as our mouths homed in on each other, tongues once again playing silkily together. I noted the astonishing coppery taste of my blood mixed with something so incredibly sweet and was sure I'd never get enough.

Even though I asked many questions, she provided no answers, and in the morning I awoke to find her gone and the cave empty. Even the bats had left me all alone. I got dressed and found a note on the table.

Antonia,

Last night was amazing. I've been waiting for someone like you for a very long time. I will return at sunset and hope you will too. Follow the path I've left for you out of the cave. Te amo y adoro.

C.

Caliana? Or was it C for *Camazotz?* The more I thought of the night I spent with her, the more it all seemed like a dream, but as I touched the pulsating mark on the side of my neck I knew there was no doubt. Yes, I would be back. I needed her now just as much as she needed me. It was the law of the Camazotz, after all, and most importantly, of my heart.

THE POND

D. Jackson Leigh

Willie Greyson sat on the weathered dock and extended her long legs out over the water. She dipped her heels, then immersed her feet in the sun-warmed pond. She wiggled her toes and frowned.

It seemed like she'd spent a lifetime at this small oasis hidden on the back part of Lori's father's farm, a lifetime of long minutes waiting for Lori to appear on the path across from the dock. They'd begun meeting here when they were just girls, Lori's hair in pigtails and Willie's in a single long braid. They were best friends. Willie fished and Lori talked. Damn, she could talk the paint off the side of a barn.

Then things changed. While Willie grew tall and lanky, Lori remained petite, her body softened with lush, womanly curves. Their relationship changed, too.

They discovered they wanted more.

Their first kiss had been at the beach. She'd borrowed Papa's truck and they spent the day sitting on the sand and wading in the surf hand in hand. They explored a rock outcropping, then stopped to rest in the secluded shade of a large boulder. They sat shoulder to shoulder and Lori trembled against her. It was much too warm to be chilled, but Willie wrapped an arm around her shoulders and pulled her closer. Lori looked up, their faces a hairsbreadth apart. Before Willie had time to change her mind, she lowered her head and kissed her. Lori's lips were soft and warm and tasted faintly of the salt spray.

She drove home with Lori pressed against her side, until she pulled off onto a tractor path near Lori's house and stole another long, exploring kiss. That kiss left her breathless and hungry. But for what? Did other women have the same feelings for each other? She instinctively knew this was something they must hide, but it didn't stop them.

The kiss was followed by weeks, months, of more stolen kisses, tentative touches and frustrated partings.

Willie wanted more.

She had a pretty good idea what "more" meant after one of their long make-out sessions had led her to a stunning discovery. She'd been confused by the dampness in her crotch afterward and surprised when it reappeared that night as she lay in bed and relived their kisses. She smoothed her hand down her belly and slid her fingers into her stiff curls. Yes, she was wet again. Was she ill? She didn't feel bad. In fact, it felt pretty good, really good when her fingers slid across her swollen tissue. A few more strokes and she experienced her first toe-curling, eye-opening orgasm. Wow. What had she done? Could she make it happen again? Did Lori know about this?

"More" became her new mission.

Lori was so beautiful. One look as she appeared at the edge of the pond's clearing and Willie wanted to bury her fingers in her thick mahogany curls. She wanted to stare into those sable-brown eyes framed by long, dark lashes and soak up the strength and shy affection she saw there. She wanted to feather kisses across the freckles that dotted Lori's otherwise flawless skin and to taste those soft lips.

She wanted that, but today she planned to have more.

Lori paused and their eyes locked. Willie was already wet from the anticipation, and seeing Lori standing in the sunlight, barefoot and clothed only in a simple sleeveless gingham dress, made her stand to relieve the uncomfortable pressure building in her loins. The wood dock was hot against her bare feet as she trotted to the pond's grassy bank and skirted the water to meet Lori under a huge shade oak.

Willie kissed her shyly, and the question in Lori's eyes told Willie that her nervousness was showing.

"I brought a blanket and I swiped a jar of Papa's scuppernong wine," she said.

Lori smiled at the small feast Willie had spread out for them—wine, cheese and soda crackers—and they sat with the food between them.

"Oh, Willie, this is wonderful. You won't get in trouble for the wine, will you?"

Willie grinned at her. "No, but one of my brothers might. Papa would never believe I did it."

Lori shook her head, but smiled. "You're such a scamp. Your poor brothers, always taking the blame."

"They've all done it before, so they'll be too busy blaming each other to think it could be me." She uncapped the mason jar, handed it to Lori and watched her take a sip.

"It's sweet," Lori said.

"Sweet like you." Willie followed Lori's pink tongue swiping across her lips to gather all of the grapes' nectar. Her cheeks heated when she realized Lori caught her staring, and she began to ramble nervously. "It won a blue ribbon at the county fair last year. Papa says this year's batch is even better, and he's going to enter the fair again next month."

Lori handed the jar back to Willie and lowered her eyes, toying with the hem of her dress.

Willie frowned. "What's the matter? Is the wine too sweet?"

"No, the wine is perfect." She looked at Willie, affection softening her gaze. "You're perfect." Her expression turned to frustration. "It's just that, well, Earl Montgomery asked Daddy if he could take me to the fair next month. I told Daddy I was going with you, but Mama said it's time for me to start paying some attention to boys."

Willie took a big gulp of the wine and swallowed it down. "Is that what you want to do?" She stared at the blanket and picked at a loose thread near her knee.

"No." Lori crawled around the food and took Willie's face in her hands. "I want to go with you, Willie."

Willie searched her eyes and saw the truth of her declaration. "I told Papa that I don't want to get married. I want to go to the university and get a degree and then a good job. I'll buy a house and you can come live with me. They'll call us old maids, but I don't care. I just want to be with you. I love you, Lori."

Lori's eyes filled. "I love you, too, Willie. Only you."

Her lips, her tongue, tasted of the wine and Willie drank her in. She gathered Lori in her arms and eased her down until they were lying side by side. She was careful, though. Lori's tiny, delicate frame always made her feel big and clumsy. But Lori rolled onto her back and drew Willie down on top of her.

"I'll crush you," she murmured.

"No, you won't," Lori said. "I love the weight of your body on mine. I love your strength."

Willie kissed her way down Lori's neck and sucked at her

pulse because she'd discovered that it made Lori hum with pleasure. She hummed now and Willie reflexively pressed her tingling crotch against Lori's hip. She captured Lori's mouth, pouring all the passion, all the feeling that was welling up in her, into a long kiss as she inched her hand up to cup Lori's breast. They'd done this before, and Willie anticipated Lori's whimper when she circled her thumb around the rigid bump of her nipple.

She broke their kiss and stared into Lori's eyes as she slowly unbuttoned her dress. They hadn't done this before. They'd only groped and pressed together fully clothed. But Lori didn't stop her. Instead, she reached for the buttons of Willie's shirt, too.

Lori's chest was flushed, but her skin was cool. Willie slipped her hand under the stiff white cotton of Lori's bra, then closed her eyes and moaned at the supple flesh that filled her palm.

"Oh, Willie." Lori wiggled beneath her. "Let me up."

"I'm sorry, I'm sorry." She withdrew her hand and sat up abruptly. "I didn't mean—"

"No, it's okay." Lori sat up, too. "I just—" She unfastened the last button on Willie's shirt and dropped her gaze to take her in.

Willie had never needed to wear a bra under the work shirts she always wore. She was glad for that now. She shivered when Lori pushed the shirt back and trailed her fingertips lightly across her collarbone, then downward to touch her small breasts.

"So strong, but so soft," Lori said, pushing the shirt off Willie's shoulders. She stopped. "Is this okay?"

"Yes."

"I want…I want to feel your skin on mine, Willie. Take this off and unhook my bra for me."

Willie shucked off her shirt and leaned into Lori, kissing her again as she reached around to work the hooks loose and pull the straps from Lori's shoulders. Lori lay back and drew Willie down with her. Their moans mingled as their breasts brushed together.

"Willie." Lori's hands explored her back, her arms tightening around her.

Willie kissed her again. Their tongues danced sensuously, then desperately.

Lori squirmed. "Willie, god." Her tone went from breathless to desperate. "I want...I want—"

Willie knew what Lori wanted. "More," she said, smoothing her fingertips along Lori's cheek. "I want it, too. Do you trust me to show you?"

Lori trembled. "Yes. Yes, please, before I break into a million pieces from wanting you."

No one ever came to the pond except them, so Willie didn't hesitate as she rolled onto her back and unbuckled her belt. She could feel Lori watching as she stripped off her jeans and underpants, and when she rolled to face her again, Lori was wiggling out of her panties, too.

Clothes cast aside, no barriers between them, they both stared. Willie thought she was going to faint at the sight of Lori completely naked, then she remembered to breathe. "You are so beautiful," she whispered.

"Show me," Lori said softly.

She bent her head to taste Lori's lips, then her neck and chest. She flicked her tongue against one pink nipple, and Lori arched upward.

"Harder, Willie." Her hands were on Willie's breasts, massaging and tweaking her sensitive nipples. "Harder like this."

Willie gently bit the nipple in her mouth and cupped Lori's other breast with her hand, lightly pinching. She smiled at her shy little Lori's full-throated moan.

She slipped her leg between Lori's thighs. Lori was slick and hot, and Willie groaned at the pleasure of knowing they were together in their desire. She kept teasing Lori's breast with her hand, but rose to claim her mouth again. Her hips bucked and her sex slid easily against Lori's leg as their tongues moved together. Holy Mother, that felt good. Too good. Another stroke, and she'd be beyond holding back.

She skimmed Lori's soft belly to part her folds, and Lori whimpered as Willie found her swelling flesh. She'd had some practice now with her own body and used that knowledge to find the spot that made Lori wrench away from their kiss and gasp. She was careful to keep the pressure light, but it was difficult. Lori's thigh pushed harder into Willie's crotch, making it almost impossible to concentrate as her own need rode her hard, racing against her determination to bring Lori to orgasm first.

Lori sucked in an abrupt breath and her eyes widened. "Oh, god, Willie, oh." Lori's body bowed beneath her, and Willie gave in to her own climax.

She didn't remember rolling onto her back and pulling Lori on top of her, but she was thankful. Her heart surely would have pounded right out of her chest if it wasn't for Lori's cheek pressed against it. They panted, perspiration sheening their naked bodies.

Lori shuddered, her body tensing and releasing with the residual of her climax. Her words were a breathy whisper. "I never knew."

"Yeah. Me neither." Willie stroked Lori's back, still marveling at the intimacy of touching her bare skin. She chuckled. "I sort of found out by accident one night after you got me all worked up with your kisses."

Lori lifted her head to hold her gaze. "I love you, Willie."

"I love you, Lori, more than I thought I could love anyone. It makes me crazy to think about you being with anyone else."

"I'll never love anyone but you."

Willie hugged her tightly and swore she'd never let Lori go. They'd find a way to be together.

"Lorraine?"

They both jerked up as Lori's mother called out.

"Where are you?" Her voice came from the edge of the clearing.

"Shit." Willie looked for their scattered clothes.

"There's no time." Lori's eyes were wide with panic.

"Jump in the pond."

They both ran to the water and dove in. When they surfaced, Mrs. Caulder was standing next to their blanket.

"Lorraine Caulder, what on earth?"

Lori bobbed in the water. "We were just swimming to cool off, Mama. Is something wrong?"

Mrs. Caulder stared down at their picnic and scattered clothes. "I'll tell you what's wrong." She put her hands on her hips and gave Willie a murderous glare that made her want to duck back under the water. "Your tomboy days of traipsing around the woods and skinny-dipping are over. You are much too old, young lady."

"But, Mama—"

"No buts, Lorraine. Get up to the house. Now."

Lori gave Willie a beseeching look.

"Go ahead," Willie said, her voice low. She was beyond miserable that their perfect afternoon had been shattered, but Lori's dilemma was what mattered. "I'll talk to you tomorrow."

Lori swam to the shore and quickly dressed. When she turned back to Willie, Mrs. Caulder swatted her on the butt. "Git. Now. Earl Montgomery has come calling and is waiting in the parlor.

You need to get cleaned up before he sees you looking like a wild ragamuffin."

Willie lifted her hand in a silent wave when Lori glanced back for one last look before disappearing down the path.

Mrs. Caulder lingered, glaring at Willie until she wondered if the woman expected her to get out of the water and dress in front of her.

"Y'all aren't children anymore, and you need to leave my daughter alone." She looked down at the blanket, and Willie felt suddenly exposed, as if Lori's mother could see what they had been doing. Her eyes were hard when she looked up at Willie again. "I don't want to talk to your parents, but I will if you come around again."

Willie stood in the water for a long time after Mrs. Caulder left. She was scared, really scared. Could they keep her from seeing Lori? She waded out of the pond and dressed. Lori loved her. They would find a way to be together.

She waited at the pond every day for three long weeks—the worst weeks of her life. She closed her eyes against the hollow ache that slowly choked her as she sat on the dock every day, waiting, wondering, and waiting more.

Desperate, she finally went to Lori's house, determined to talk to her. They could run away to another town and get jobs. She didn't have to go to the university. She'd do anything as long as she didn't lose Lori.

But when she walked into the yard, she could hear the angry voices inside. She knocked, but no one came to the door. She knocked again, and Lori finally appeared. Her eyes were red from crying, and she refused to look at Willie as she told her that she was going to marry Earl Montgomery next month.

Willie hung around until the day of the wedding and stood across the street from the church. When Lori arrived, she got out of the car and looked right at Willie, then walked into the sanctuary. Willie drove to the bus station, bought a ticket to Richmond and joined the army.

She never thought she'd find herself back at this pond, waiting once again for Lori. She squinted in the bright sunlight, searching the tree line again as if she could will her to appear. Every moment without her still seemed like a millennium.

Army life had been good to her, but even sweeter was their reunion and the years they'd finally spent together. The years of waiting had been more than worth it. So there was no doubt that she would wait for Lori again…as long as it took. But then time had no relevance here in this oasis that was theirs.

The water shimmered around her and Willie closed her eyes against the glare. When she opened them, Lori stood on the bank across from her. Her smile was soft. "Somehow, I knew I'd find you here."

Willie sprang to her feet and dove into the water, swimming across the small pond in strong, sure strokes. Lori waded in to meet her and they were in each other's arms again. Lori's kiss was as sweet as she remembered.

Then Lori's hands were on Willie's face, smoothing down her shoulders and arms to cup Willie's hands in her smaller ones and examine them. She felt her own face, then looked up at Willie in wonderment.

"We're young again."

"Yes." Willie held up her hands. "No more arthritis."

"I never minded. I was too glad to find you after all those years apart."

"I never expected I would go first. Was it hard after I left?"

"It was dark and confusing. Poor Leah. I don't know what my granddaughter would have done without your great-niece to love her and help her through it."

"Tory is stronger with Leah at her side, too."

Lori nodded. "They'll be fine." She smiled. "Did you have to wait long this time, sweetheart? I couldn't keep track of the days. The dementia stole that from me, but sometimes I thought it was actually a gift because it kept me from knowing how long I was without you."

"It doesn't matter how long. I would wait all of eternity for you."

Lori looked around. "So, this is heaven? No angels or choirs? No judgment of our sins?"

"Are you disappointed?"

"Heavens, no. I'm relieved."

They laughed together, and Willie stole another kiss.

"Apparently, we must have done something right. Our eternity will be spent in the place where we shared our happiest memory." She gestured toward her offerings under the gnarled old oak.

Lori's smile went from sweet to brilliant. "Oh, Willie. In all the years I've loved you, I'm glad you never changed."

Willie winked at Lori. "I brought a blanket and a jar of Papa's scuppernong wine."

AUSSIE GIRL

Jillian Boyd

Saturday afternoon, half past one.

I sat near the window at Starbucks, getting better acquainted with a latte. The weather gods were not being kind. Outside, the people of Chelmsford rushed about the street, clad in their macs and wellies.

I really shouldn't have bothered. "Dylan from work" obviously hadn't. Couldn't blame her, though. I mean, in this day and age, who the fuck agrees to a blind date anymore? Oh yeah, I did.

It was all Mel's fault, really. "I work with a lovely girl. You should meet her! You two would get on like a house on fire! Come on, you need a bit of flirting in your life!"

I agreed, mostly to get Mel off my back. Knowing my luck, "a lovely girl" would mean that she was a bit of a bitch who was quite possibly a racist, but perfectly okay when you meet her at the water cooler.

The minutes ticked over to two o'clock. Still no sight of the mysterious Dylan. I sighed and stood up from my seat.

Suddenly, I felt a light tap on my shoulder.

"Excuse me. Are you Sara?"

I turned around to see a young woman fiddling with the wet hem of her skirt. I felt my lips curl into a smile and my breath hitch in my throat.

"Yes. I really hope you're Dylan," I said.

"Yes! Oh, thank god, I thought Mel made you up."

A tiny spark made my belly fizz. She was absolutely stunning. I uttered a quick thank you to Mel.

"No. I'm very real. Come, sit down."

Dylan sat down and took a gulp of her coffee. "Is this supposed to be summer, then?" she said, looking out the window.

"Yeah, it's quite depressing," I said, homing in on her ample cleavage. I could feel my cheeks burning.

"I miss a bit of sunshine." She sighed. "Only, I miss home when it's pissing down like this."

"Where are you from?"

"The Land Down Under. I'm a true Aussie girl."

Only then did I realize that her accent seemed completely different from the Essex twang. "Oh! I love Australia! Didgeridoos and kangaroos and whatnot!"

Dylan chuckled. "Well, there are some of those about."

"I'm sorry. It's basically all I know about Australia. I'd love to go someday, but with slightly more knowledge."

And a ravishing, ample-bosomed guide to take me there.

"Well, you seem like a top sheila. What do you want to know?"

We drank our coffees and talked about life in Australia versus life in Essex. I couldn't stop looking at her plump, rosy lips. Hooked on her every word. What was such a beautiful, worldly girl doing in Essex of all places?

"Oh, you know. Mate of mine had a flat here, and I wanted to get away from Brisbane. It was a start. Plus, Chelmsford's nice."

"Have you seen the sights here?"

"Well, there's not much to be seen! But..."

A glint in her eye made my belly feel like it had been invaded by butterflies.

"I'd like to see the cathedral."

"Oh. Right. It's not that exciting, you know."

"Yeah, I know. But it's the company I'm in that makes it more exciting."

I flushed red and decided that if she wanted to see the cathedral, she was going to get a damn good tour of the place, regardless of how much of a non-event it was.

Trying to decipher the old gravestones in the courtyard had proven to be quite a task. Dylan looked over my shoulder as I gave it another go. The sun had reappeared with a vengeance and I could feel tiny rivulets of moist sweat forming on my forehead.

"B...E...J... Em, I have no idea," I said, plonking down on the grass.

"Good, because I have no idea too. How old are these?"

"Probably hundreds of years old."

"Hmm. Imagine being alive back then. No fun to be had anywhere."

"True. We probably would be frowned upon."

"Of course. All the cool people would be frowned upon. You were only allowed to be a boring tit. No freedom of expression, sexuality was a moot point.... It wouldn't be fun."

With that, she grabbed my hand and placed a kiss on the palm. "But luckily, we live in different times."

She snuggled up against me, and my belly fizzed again.

We moved on and ventured to a sex shop near the station. Dylan had to pull me inside, red-faced and nervous. The man at the counter frowned at the sight of a sprightly Aussie lass, bouncing about.

I marveled at her wonder at everything in stock. She gasped as she eagerly fingered the leather corsets, lace underthings and bottles of lube.

And then she found a bright pink double-ender dildo. "How the hell is this supposed to go in anything?" she said.

I furrowed my brows at the neon monster. "You could use it as a doorstop."

"Or for a friendly game of dildo jousting!"

"What the hell is that?"

"Swordfighting with dildos. Hurts much, much less. Although I wouldn't know with this one." She swished and swooshed the dildo about, and my composure failed me. I broke out into a giggle.

We left in a hurry, holding hands, nearly forgetting to put down the dildo.

"There's a lot of pigeons here," she said. We had ended up in the Central Park, sitting cross-legged on the grass. Dylan fiddled with flowers.

"Yeah. Chelmsford has a high pigeon turnover."

She chuckled, which made me chuckle. "It's something to be very proud of," she said, nodding earnestly.

I stretched and lay back on the grass, letting the warm sun cradle me. Dylan followed suit and swung her arm around my waist.

"So, am I making a good impression?"

I turned to look into her eyes. "I'm not regretting showing up anymore."

"Good. I like you too. And I kinda want to do something."

"What do you want to do?"

Before I knew it, Dylan grabbed me and kissed me squarely on the lips. It lasted three full seconds, but I could have gone on forever. My breath caught in my throat again, and I could feel my cunt trembling.

"Test the waters."

She grinned like a little minx.

We made plans for dinner the next week. As we said good-bye, Dylan leaned in and whispered, "You're a sexy girl, you know."

I watched her walk away. No, scratch that, I watched her skip away, giggling.

The next few days were spent compulsively checking my phone. Every text made my heart leap into my throat. Every word turned me on. I didn't want to fuck it up. I wanted her.

I discussed it with Mel, over coffee.

"So. I set you up on a date...and it worked?" she said, eating carrot cake.

"Yes, Mel, I've told you three times now."

"I know. It's just so surprising. Anyway, what are you worrying about? She likes you and you clearly like her, seeing as you've been fiddling with your phone for the last half hour."

"I don't know!" I said, guiltily putting my phone away. "I just want this to go right. I don't want to be all...googly moogly."

Mel peered at me. "Define googly moogly?"

"Never mind. I just don't want to fuck this up. I rarely get a second chance."

"Sara, you have nothing to worry about. Dylan likes you. Trust me."

I didn't trust Mel for a mile. Standing outside the restaurant, I checked my phone, eager for a message. Nothing.

* * *

I knew this would happen. I knew she'd back out and leave me here like a wally. Sighing, I tucked my phone away and turned to leave, when I felt a tap on my shoulder.

"What are you doing outside, silly?"

There she was: Dylan, all smiles. My stomach burst into a flutter of butterflies. She came. She came!

"You didn't think I'd stand you up, right?" she said.

"I actually did. Sad, isn't it?"

"Well, I'm here. Let's get food."

The restaurant was busy, as usual.

"Now that I'm here, I have no idea what to eat," I said, secretly thinking that there was one thing I would love to devour....

"We should order everything on the menu, really."

"I'm not that rich, love."

"Neither am I. But imagine doing that, though. You'd be full for weeks."

"I wouldn't be able to walk. Or function in general."

She grinned, taking my hand in hers. I relaxed into my seat and a happy sigh escaped me.

Eventually, the waiter came to take our order. Over pizza, we shared bits and bobs of our lives.

"My sister was supportive of me coming out," I said. "Parents, bit weird about it. Turned out all right in the end, though."

"My parents were iffy too. They came around, though. Guess we were the lucky ones."

I nodded, trying to concentrate on my food. All I could focus on was her. I didn't want this night to end.

On the way back home, I kept asking myself questions. All of them reverted to the same answer. *Yes, I want her!* My heart pounded out a hard-assed beat and my pussy seemed made out of liquid longing. Dylan obviously sensed something was up, because as we arrived at my front door, she turned to me and gave me a peck on the cheek.

"Well, I'll be going, then."

Fuck. She'd sensed wrongly. She pulled herself away and was about to walk off when I grabbed her arm and pulled her close, crushing my lips against hers and taking possession of her mouth. She gave in and kissed me back, pressing her body into mine. I could feel something hard pressing against my leg and deduced that she had come prepared.

"Take me upstairs. Now."

The tension that had been building all night came to a rushing high as I dragged Dylan into the bedroom and threw her onto the bed. All I wanted was to fuck her, to be fucked by her, to completely lose my head in the throes of pleasure.

Dylan's lipstick smeared all over my face as she kissed and undressed me at the same time. The blood rushed everywhere, and I could feel my clit pulsing a frantic beat. The summer heat blazed through the room and the smell of sex and sweat made my nostrils tingle.

The sight of her nearly naked body drove me insane. Clad in a harness with a shiny pink dildo perched on the front, she took control.

"Lube?"

"Bedside table."

I watched as she rummaged through my drawer and pulled out a half-empty bottle of Liquid Silk. She giggled as I blushed.

"Been fiddling much lately?"

"Well, I've not been having sex lately, so a fiddle or two is a must, I think."

"Clever girl." Dylan straddled me and grabbed my hips,

slowly brushing the tip of her pink menace against my wet slit. "Spread for me, just a little more."

I did as told, and the head of the dildo rested temptingly against my entrance. When she entered me, I gasped.

"Gosh, that's a big thing," I managed to utter.

She giggled. "I thought you might like it."

She began to move, resting her hands on my hips. My eyes closed with pleasure as I rubbed my clit against the base of the dildo. She threw her head back and moaned.

"Bloody hell!"

Her thrusting sped up, intermixed with kisses and caresses. I clawed my fingers into her back as her breasts pressed against mine. I wrapped my legs around her waist, letting her in deeper, thrusting back and making her moan even harder.

"Christ, you're going to give me friction burn," she said with a throaty chuckle. But then words escaped her as she moaned again, in time with me. I wrapped my arm around her shoulders and rested my head against them. My hand snaked toward her beautiful breasts. I could feel her heartbeat quickening.

"God, don't stop," I cried out.

Her cock pressed against me, against her. She went faster and faster and sweat dripped over our bodies and moans filled the air.

"I think I'm coming," she whispered.

I grabbed her arse and pushed her into me, feeling my own climax in time with hers. A shiver ran down my spine as she relaxed on top of me.

"You look beautiful when you come." Dylan pressed a kiss to my forehead. I could only sigh. She held me and whispered sweet nothings in my ear until we were both too tired to do anything else but sleep.

In the morning, I woke up before her. I watched the morning sun illuminate her pale skin, a smile playing on her face. And just like that, I felt the first stirrings of love.

A bit early, but who could blame me? I'd found my Aussie girl.

PINK LADY FRIENDS

Allison Wonderland

"Duck...duck...goose!"

I make good on my word, directing my pointer finger toward the unsuspecting posterior in front of me.

"Ow! Leslie!" Ramona yelps. "What is the matter with you, you little stinker?" she demands, hands on hips. The hips are hers, but the hands belong to me.

"So typical," I comment, smiling until she does. "I cop a feel and you cop an attitude. Don't be afraid to take frisks. You know what they say: no frisk, no reward. Isn't that right, Ramones?"

Ramona rolls her eyes. She's not exactly a fan of that band, although you'd think a musical theater junkie would have at least a marginal appreciation for *Rock 'n' Roll High School*.

Anyway, "Don't you dare downsize your derriere, got it? I like your cushy tushy. Plus, it works for Jan."

"My character is pretty fant*ass*tic, isn't she?" Ramona concurs, ushering a bevy of bobby pins into her palm.

"The fantasstic-ist. We should have a rump roast during

lunch on Monday. We'll go around the cafeteria and all your closest friends can say stuff about your duff. Good stuff, of course. Heaven forbid you become the next booty school dropout."

"You are always like this after a show," Ramona remarks, sounding at once fazed and amazed. "You're also only like this after a show. You're so bizarre, you know that?"

"Help," I shriek, clutching Ramona's arms through her satin jacket. "I've fallen off my rocker and can't get up!"

Okay, obviously she's right about me—I am bizarre. I'm a totally different person onstage than off. And not just for obvious reasons. Onstage, no matter what kind of character I'm playing, I've got nerve and verve and unquenchable confidence. But when the curtain closes and the lights come up, my shell goes right back on.

Well, not immediately. There's a brief bracket of time when the show is over but I'm not over the show—that's when I'm at my silliest and my sassiest. I love it when I'm like that, so I try to stay out-of-character for as long as possible.

"Do you think my...bizarreness is nifty or shifty?" I inquire, adjusting the flipped fluff that is my Frenchy wig. It's a cute pink color, like the nose on a stuffed bunny. Or the nipples under a stuffed bra.

Not that Ramona stuffs her bra. Anymore. She and the socks had a bit of a falling-out in the seventh grade and after that, she—

"I think it's nifty," Ramona is saying as she holds my wig stand steady. She fondles my fingers a little and I look up, then down when her brassiere comes into view in all its unstuffed glory. "Now your eyes, on the other hand—those are kind of shifty. Are you going to stand there gawking like a fangirl while I get changed?"

"I thought you liked it when all eyes are on you."

"I do, especially when they're all yours."

When she gets gushy, I get mushy, and right now, my insides are gooier than s'mores.

Ramona reaches for my hand. I let her take it. If there was anyone else in here, even one of our nearest and dearest, I'd follow the first rule of kindergarten: hands to selves, please. But in their haste to get to the cast party, the other girls did a quick change into their street clothes after the performance. This is the advantage of being a slowpoke—we have the dressing room all to ourselves. And Ramona takes just as much time as I do transforming from starlet to your everyday gay.

"I like holding your hand," I muse, enjoying the cozy cushion of Ramona's palm and the gentle pressure of her lavender-frosted fingers.

"Me, too," Ramona says, and smiles her picture-day smile.

"I always knew you could hold your own. I just didn't think you'd want to."

Ramona giggles and rubs her nose against mine and in that brief bit of friction, I feel our signature spark. "The only thing I don't want to do is strike the set tomorrow," the diva laments. "I hate saying good-bye to Rydell High." Ramona frowns then, her brow pleating like a paper fan.

"What?"

She drops my hand. "You made me rhyme," she flouts, and pouts. "This is the end of the beginning. We've officially entered that stage of coupledom where we become adorably and disgustingly interchangeable." She pauses, looking at me like...I don't know, like she's looking for something. I just hope she finds what she's looking for.

Now she's looking for something else—inside her shoulder bag. "Now may or may not be a good time to give you this," she says, and hands me a folded tee as square as Sandra Dee. "But it's as good a time as any."

I unfold the garment and hold it out in front of me. It's a black T-shirt with hot pink text traveling across the front.

I'm not a lesbian, says the shirt, *but my girlfriend is.*

"I'm a lesbian," I insist, in a decidedly dull roar.

Well, I am. And I'm out and proud—to myself, my parents, my...well, I guess the only other person currently on that list is my girlfriend, and I know she'd like it if I were...outer. I'm not really sure why I've been so reluctant to reveal our relationship to our peers. Maybe it's my aversion to aspersion, a rational fear of bullying. Maybe it's because I prefer to fade into the background when I'm not in the spotlight.

Maybe it's the fact that theater is a gay man's world. If a guy's into drama, people just assume he's gay, right? Not that that's a good thing, but what about those thespians who are lesbians, like Ramona and me? If anyone's looking for us, we'll be in the Dyke Drama Department, established...well, not yet established.

I just wish I could be as cool with it as she is. People know Ramona's gay—I mean, when they ask, she tells. Like, when a guy asks her out, she'll come right out and say she's not into guys. Of course, not everyone believes her, because she doesn't "look" gay—whatever that means anymore, although apparently it still means something.

I think it means that unless we drop the BFF act and start acting honestly—walking the hallways hand in hand, sharing smooches and moony, swoony looks—no one will know what we mean to each other.

"Hey, Ramones, how come you're so...out there?"

She shrugs casually, but her ego trips the light fantastic. "Just call me Ramona the Brave."

"Ramona the Brave, why do you tolerate me?" We've been going steady for an entire semester. How much guile can one put up with after a while?

She shrugs again, a sign that she's resigned to this. "Just hopelessly devoted, I suppose. I don't press the issue because it'll just make things tense and awkward. The more we fret together, the unhappier we'll be."

"I see."

"No, you don't," Ramona counters, and passes me my glasses.

I don't need them. I can see Ramona quite queerly.

My head starts spinning like a pinwheel, the colors whirring and blurring into a bewildered rainbow. "Look, I know I'm not worthy, but I want to be because you're the one that I want—I don't need anything but you, and I'm sick of all this cowardly lyin' and even though I'm totally mixing up my musicals right now, I mean every word, Ramones."

Ramona starts to laugh, but the look she's giving me is soft, clear, sincere. I marvel at the beauty of her authenticity.

I'm thinking of falling in love with her.

Actually, I'm thinking I already have. Our connection is... perfection is what it is. When I concentrate on that, instead of on the "consequences" of being her not-so-secret girlfriend, I realize there really aren't any. There are only perks and possibilities.

I decide to exile the denial, a.k.a. the shirt, so I toss it to the floor.

"We're going together," I announce.

"I know we are."

"To the cast party," I clarify. "We're going together."

"I know we are."

"As a couple." I try again. "We're going together as a couple.

A couple that's going together. A couple that's…a couple."

Ramona's smile is wide with pride and her eyes shine like stage lights.

I open my arms.

She closes the space.

I hug Ramona to my heart's content.

"Well, let's get going together," she chirps, loosening her grip.

Ramona dons her denim blouse and begins to button it—badly.

I giggle, feeling lucky and loopy and lovesick. I take a picture of Ramona, my eye the camera lens, and add it to the thousands of snapshots that have accumulated in my cerebral scrapbook. This one is captioned: *Don't fail to sail on that dreamboat.*

"You're magnificent," I tell her, shooting Cupid's arrows at Ramona with my eyes.

She leans forward until our foreheads are touching. "And what are you?"

A serene smile tickles my lips. "I'm yours."

"In that case, I'm glad you lost your shirt," Ramona says, glancing at the rumpled lump on the floor.

"I'd rather lose my shirt than lose you."

A grin nips at Ramona's lips, and then Ramona's lips nip at mine.

When we kiss, my whole body takes note, an ensemble of tingles all too happy to harmonize.

"Ready, Les?" Ramona asks.

She loops a lock of hair behind my ear and I slip my arm through hers so that we're linked like a magician's rings. There's a song in our show—"Those Magic Changes." I just hope I can say the same for our situation.

Revelation?

Celebration.

Yeah, celebration. That's the most optimistic option.

"Ready, Ramones," I answer. "Time for our relationship to take center stage."

When we make the scene, we make an entrance: my arm around her waist, her arm around mine.

I can do this. No big deal. No sweat—except on my palms.

"Come on, snake," Ramona says. "Let's rattle."

"Are you asking me to dance?"

"Duh, dummy." Coming from her, it sounds like a term of endearment.

She leads me through the throng of thespians convened in the converted basement of the school's Drama Queen (our director and favorite acting teacher), and we exchange greetings and congratulations with our cast mates.

No one cares how couple-y we look. Either that or no one notices, which, I have to admit, bugs me a bit.

What do we have to do, put a bug in someone's ear?

Apparently. After a dozen dances, including a few slow ones, not one cast member has cast an eyeball at us.

I guess we'll have to show *and* tell to get through to these folks.

"I'm twist-and-shouted out," Ramona announces midway through the shindig. "I'll grab some punch and you grab a seat."

"Okay," I say, my hand heading toward her heinie.

"Get away from my party pooper!" Ramona giggle-shrieks, and tips me into an inelegant dip.

Doody enters, as if on cue (ewww), accompanied by Roger, Jan's love interest. That's funny—I don't recall asking where the boys are. They're nice and all, but during rehearsals, I got the feeling that they were hoping life would imitate art and a "showmance" would develop.

"They've entered right and left," Ramona whispers, and I try to ignore the warm welcome her breath brings to my ear. "Actually—and unfortunately—they haven't left."

"You girls were awesome," says Roger. Real name: Rob, as in I'm-stealing-your-girlfriend, although in all fairness, I'm sure he doesn't consider it stealing since he has no idea that I've already stolen Ramona's heart.

A slow song comes on: "I Love How You Love Me," a gender-neutral girl-group great.

Doody, more eloquently known as Jack, inquires, "May I have this dance?" He extends his hand. Take it or leave it.

I leave it. "I'm taken."

"With me, I hope."

"By her, you dope."

"What, are you gay or something?" Jack chuckles. It's not mean-spirited, but my heart still feels like it's jumping on a moon bounce.

Ramona looks at me. I look at Ramona, who looks more hopeful than expectant. I take a deep breath. An order of oxygen with a side of courage—and make it snappy.

"As a matter of fact," I reply, and push my glasses up the bridge of my nose, because that's what bespectacled people do when we mean business, "I'm gay *and* I'm something." I hitch my hand to Ramona's. "This is my girlfriend," I continue. "She's something else."

"She's also as gay as a lady is pink," Ramona adds, our joined hands swinging to and fro like a swishy poodle skirt.

"Unreal," Rob remarks. In the '50s, that meant exceptional, so we'll take that as a compliment.

"That's the word from the bird," Ramona affirms, and we watch as the dejected duo departs. "May *I* have this dance?" She extends her hand. Take it or else.

I take it.

We sway together, huddled in a cuddle, because I don't need a Jack in my box or in my arms.

"Leslie, I have so much gay pride in you right now, it's not even funny."

"Just call me Leslie the Lesbo."

"Leslie the Lesbo, I love you." The declaration is delicate, decisive, definitive. The words barely hover before they cover my heart, which proceeds to melt into a giant puddle of fondue. Meanwhile, my eyes have started to water, but I don't mind, because on a queer day, you can see forever. And right now, I can see myself with her forever, and—

Oh, boy. It's official. This girl totally Ram-owns me.

"I love you, too," I ditto without further delay.

"You love U2? I thought you were all about the Ramones."

"Oh, I *am* all about the Ramones."

The distance between us dwindles, the frenzy of freckles on Ramona's nose getting fainter; the scent of her hair, a duet of almonds and oranges, getting stronger.

"Don't be afraid to take risks," she whispers, kissably close. "No risk, no reward. Right, Lesbo?"

My breath zigzags in my throat.

"I could care less what people think," Ramona reminds me. "Could you?"

"I...could care less, too."

"Then do it. Care less. And kiss more."

I give her first a half-smile and then a whole one and now I'm tilting my head for a meet-and-greet with her mouth. I pursue the pressure of Ramona's lips and discover, to my surprise, that I thrive under pressure.

I also discover, to my surprise, that no one flips or flips out or offers us a knuckle sandwich. Nobody gives a hoot and only a handful give a holler: an LOL here, an OMG there, and the rest are all in "awww." Those kooky kids.

The slow song segues into something speedier: an oldie by the Knack.

"I love this song!" Ramona announces, and bounces.

So I serenade her, my voice vacillating between shy and sweet and loud and proud. I hope she can hear my rendition over everyone else's and I especially hope that she takes it personally.

"M-m-m-my Ramona!"

Let's broadcast it to the world.

Well, today the theater world.

Tomorrow, the whole world.

So look out, world, 'cause queer we come.

SECOND CHANCES

Jade Melisande

Abigail slowed to a walk and finally came to a stop at a cross-roads, pulling the cap from her head and gloves from her hands one by one as she brought her breathing under control and felt her heart rate slow. Her breath billowed from her mouth in vaporous clouds and condensation formed on her sunglasses, which she removed as well. She put an arm around first one knee and then the other, pulling them up high against her chest to give her hamstrings and glutes a good stretch before they cooled down too much. In response, a muscle spasmed in her ass. She groaned and reached back to massage it.

"Need some help with that?"

Abigail spun around to find the owner of the voice grinning at her: a tall, slender woman with dark hair pulled back in a ponytail, large grayish-green eyes and a mischievous grin. Unlike Abigail, who wore her typical running gear, the woman was in hip-hugging jeans, boots with *actual* spurs (though not the sharp pointy kind in cowboy movies, Abigail noted) and a long-sleeved T-shirt that stretched across full breasts and well-defined arms. A cowboy hat topped her ensemble, shading a face Abigail guessed had seen a few less summers than hers, though not many.

"Hi," Abigail said uncertainly. Had this woman just offered to massage her ass? She'd never been hit on by a woman before. If that was what was happening.

She gave herself a mental shake. Of course that couldn't be what the woman was suggesting. She had to have been joking. Of course she was joking.

"Um, thanks," she said, "but I've got it under control." She lifted her leg and hugged it to her chest again to get the maximum stretch. The woman stepped forward and placed a hand on Abigail's shin, exerting gentle pressure on it, presumably to help Abigail with her stretch.

Presumably.

Abigail met the woman's eyes, only inches from her own. She felt the warmth and firmness of the woman's hand on her leg and saw a hint of that same grin she'd given her moments before lift the corner of her mouth. Her breath caught in her throat and the place where the woman held her leg suddenly felt hypersensitive.

"Thank...thank you," she said, dropping her leg and stepping back.

The woman stuck out her hand. "I'm Laura," she said.

Abigail took it in her own. "Abigail," she replied. The woman's hand was firm and strong, yet delicately boned. And warm. Abigail wondered when the last time was that she had held a woman's hand.

She pulled her hand away abruptly. This wasn't hand-holding, this was hand-shaking. She felt her face heat and looked down in embarrassment and some confusion.

"Nice to meet you, Abigail," the woman said. "Are you vacationing around here?"

Abigail looked up at her. Her smile was generous, inviting, and Abigail found herself warm to her. "Frost Valley Resort," she said, nodding back the way she had come with her chin. "You?"

Laura chuckled. "Nope. Born and raised here," she said. "My vacations are taken in the tropics. Got to get away from real life occasionally, right?"

The thought of "real life" brought a small frown to Abigail's face. Getting away from real life was certainly what she was doing here.

"You *live* here?" she said, realizing belatedly how inane she sounded.

Laura only chuckled again. "Yes," she said, "there are a few of us that actually do."

Abigail looked around, noticing for the first time the lane she'd stopped in. It curved between rows of pines and was flanked on both sides by a tall, wooden fence, behind which she could see shaggy-coated horses grazing. A saddled horse was tethered to a fencepost just off the road.

Robert used to tell her that she was a danger when she ran, oblivious to the world around her, and she had to admit it was true. She plugged into her playlist and the world faded around her, narrowing down to just the music in her ears, her breath and her body. She never even noticed where she was until it ended and she stopped to look around and get her bearings. It was an old habit, a routine she had followed ever since she had started running years before.

She felt the familiar twinge of old pain at the thought of Robert. This was her first vacation since he had died two years earlier, her first vacation alone in at least ten years. They'd had a phase of separate travel for a few years somewhere in the middle of their twenty-seven-year marriage, but the last ten or so they had always traveled together. Now that he was gone, she was acutely glad for the memories of those last travels together—although, in the dark period just after his untimely death, she had wished she could forget everything. It hurt too much to remember. Now she was grateful for the memories, and the long, mostly happy marriage they had shared.

A soft hand touching hers brought Abigail back to the present with a start. She looked over at the woman—Laura—and realized that she had been speaking to her. "I'm sorry," Abigail said. "What did you say?"

"I asked if you've ever been horseback riding," Laura answered. "You were looking at Buck so intently," she said, nodding over at the horse. "Kind of...sadly. Or longingly." She smiled a little. "Kind of like I used to when I was a girl, wanting to ride the horses in the field next to the house I grew up in."

"Oh," Abigail began, embarrassed that her emotions had been so naked on her face. "No, I..."

She paused. She had been about to explain where her thoughts had been, then thought better of it. This woman didn't know her and certainly didn't want to hear her life story. No one knew her here. That was why she was here, after all. She just wanted to be Abigail Marshall, woman on vacation, not Abigail the widow. Laura was just being polite.

"I mean, no, I haven't ridden recently. Not since I was a teenager, actually." She remembered suddenly how horse-crazy she had been as a teenager, as so many girls were. She thought about the summer she had spent at her aunt Bernie's farm in Ohio, and how she had wished so fervently that Bernadette had been her mother instead of her own mother, June, with whom Abigail had constantly argued. She remembered riding nearly every day that summer and loving the sense of freedom she had had. Come to think of it, there had been a girl there, too. What was her name? Kinsey? Casey? Something like that.

She smiled ruefully. "I guess I outgrew horses."

Laura smiled back at her. Her eyes were clear and more green than gray, with fine lines at the corners when she smiled. She had even, white teeth and a generous mouth that seemed perpetually ready to break into a grin. Abigail found herself liking her without knowing anything about her.

"Some of us never outgrow being horse-crazy," Laura said. "Most girls transfer their crazy to boys at some point, but some of us... Well, a boy can never take the place of a good horse." She chuckled in a way that seemed to include Abigail in a private joke and that made Abigail feel oddly warm.

Unbidden, the image of Casey—she was almost sure that was her name—floated into Abigail's mind again. They'd been what, thirteen or fourteen? Casey was tall and lanky, already outgrowing her baby fat, whereas Abigail was short and still pudgy. Abigail suddenly remembered one night, "camping" out in Aunt Bernie's backyard, in which Casey had confessed to kissing a local boy, and then proceeded to demonstrate—with Abigail!—what it had been like. Casey's mouth had been hard and untutored, and her tongue, when it had darted into Abigail's mouth, had startled her so much that Abigail had yelped and jumped back, sputtering, "Ew! Gross!" Casey had been infuriated and told her she was just a baby and didn't understand sex. Looking back, Abigail wholeheartedly agreed with Casey's assessment.

Abigail realized she was looking at Laura and thinking about kissing a girl. She felt her face go hot again.

Damn, what the hell was wrong with her? She was fifty-two years old, the widow of an almost thirty-year marriage, the mother of two grown children, and a successful businesswoman. And yet everything this woman said made her blush and stammer like she was fourteen again. She looked up to see Laura looking at her bemusedly.

Abigail shook her head. "I'm sorry," she said again. "I've just run six miles. I'm afraid I'm a bit wiped out." She hoped her excuse would explain away her odd behavior.

Laura cocked her head at her. "Six miles! I'd be lucky to survive two." She paused and gave Abigail a sympathetic look. "Would you like to come up to the barn for a glass of water?" When Abigail glanced up the long, tree-lined drive, she added with a wry grin, "We can ride."

Abigail's eyes widened. "Really?" she asked. "But, well, it's been so long, I wouldn't know how." But she couldn't stop herself from smiling at the thought.

Laura grinned back at her. "It's like riding a bike," she said, reaching out and taking Abigail's hand to pull her toward the horse, which turned its head to watch them approach. "Besides, all you have to do is hold on. I'll do the rest."

Five minutes later, Abigail was, indeed, holding on, her arms wrapped around Laura's waist as she guided the gelding up the lane toward the barn. He had a gentle, rolling gait that lulled Abigail. As they rode Laura told her about the breed of horse that Buck was, a Tennessee Walker, and about the history of the breed.

Abigail only paid half attention—the other half was noticing the feel of Laura's back against her breasts, Laura's thighs against hers, the feel of her waist beneath her hands. She found herself wondering what Laura's skin would feel like beneath her fingertips and surprised herself by not suppressing that curiosity as soon as it came into her head. Riding along behind her on the horse she felt safe, even with these thoughts, and she let her mind wander. It wandered back to those first moments when she had met Laura, to the woman's teasing offer to help Abigail massage the incipient cramp in her backside, to Laura's hand on her leg and in her own hand, to the warmth and...something else...in Laura's eyes and smile when she looked at Abigail. Was she reading too much into the encounter? Was Laura just being friendly to an out-of-towner?

She felt Laura's hand rest lightly on hers where it lay on Laura's waist, for just a moment. "How you doing back there?" Laura asked. Her voice was quiet, intimate. For a brief instant Abigail longed to lay her face against Laura's back as she answered. And she longed to answer truthfully. Wonderful. She was doing wonderful, and felt more alive than she had since Robert had passed away. Alive and expectant and excited.

But of course she couldn't say any of that, not to this woman, not now.

Maybe not ever.

She was obviously reading far more into this than was real, or healthy.

"I'm great," she said. "Thank you. For the ride, and the offer. It's...an unexpected pleasure." She did lean against Laura's back then, just for a moment, smiling, before pulling hurriedly away.

Laura felt Abigail's smile against her back in that momentary contact and felt something deep and warm opening up inside her. She didn't know anything about this stranger she had met on the road, but there was something about her that fascinated her.

Oh, at first she had just been blatantly flirting and teasing. What was the harm in coming on a bit to a stranger, a vacationer? She didn't know her, and she would either react positively or not—but either way she would leave in a few days, a week tops. No skin off either of their noses. But Abigail's reaction had been such a mixture of shyness and curiosity, tinged with an inexplicable sadness, that Laura had felt a little ashamed for coming on to her at all. She felt ungainly with her, a rider with a heavy hand on a horse with a soft mouth.

At the thought of Abigail's mouth, Laura suppressed a shiver. She had seen the woman's eyes go to her mouth, seen her lips part and her breathing quicken as she had held Abigail's hand in her own for just a fraction longer than was absolutely necessary. She'd been around the block a time or two. She knew the signs, recognized that Abigail was attracted to her. But she also realized that Abigail had probably never been with a woman. Either she didn't even realize her own attraction to them, or she deliberately suppressed it. Either way, whereas Laura might normally thrill to the challenge of initiating Abigail to the pleasures of sex with her own kind, a little no-strings-attached exploration, there was something about Abigail that gave her pause, some feeling of protectiveness that held her back. But what was she protecting Abigail from? Her? Or herself?

The barn was warm and redolent with the smell of hay and horses and leather. Laura took a deep breath as she brought Buck to a halt by the tack room door, feeling as unsure and gauche as a teenager.

"Hang on," she said, and swung a leg over the gelding's neck before dropping to the ground next to him. She turned and placed a hand on Abigail's calf. It was firm and well-muscled, and she felt a tremor go through the other woman at her touch. Her own belly and groin responded instinctively, tightening and yet feeling as though she was expanding inside, all at the same time. She looked up at Abigail, wondering if she had any idea of the effect she had on her.

"Swing your leg over and slide down slowly," she said, hearing the hoarseness in her own voice.

* * *

Abigail swallowed and stared down at Laura. She felt the heat in Laura's hand on her leg and felt something unspoken move between them. She leaned forward and grabbed a handful of the horse's mane, then swung her leg over, balancing across Buck's back. She felt Laura slide her hands up her waist, steadying her, as she slid down the side of the horse to land gracefully next to him. She turned and found herself within the circle of Laura's arms.

Their eyes met. Abigail realized she was holding her breath.

Buck snorted and shifted impatiently. Abigail stumbled back against him, but Laura grabbed her arms and caught her, pulling her upright. Abigail gasped as her momentum carried her forward and thrust her against Laura's chest. Laura's arms tightened instinctively, holding Abigail close.

The moment stretched, giving Abigail forever to notice the hardness of Laura's arms—and the softness of her breasts. She felt her own nipples hardening against Laura's, felt the tightness of her runner's jersey constricting them, and a flood of heat flashed through her. It blazed its way from the tips of her breasts down to the vee between her legs before it found its way back up her chest to her neck and into her face. Laura's hands left her arms and landed on her waist, then came back up to her shoulders and, finally, to the sides of her neck. She looked up into Laura's face and knew that Laura was going to kiss her.

"Laura?" The voice, strident and demanding, came from outside the open barn door. Laura merely looked in that direction, but Abigail jumped away from her and turned her face into the placid gelding's neck.

"Abigail—" Laura began.

"Laura, are you here? I need help saddling Pharo." The owner of the voice came into view. She was a pimply preteen with sandy blond hair and a petulant set to her mouth. Abigail looked over her shoulder at Laura.

Laura shrugged and turned up a corner of her mouth in what could have been amusement—or derision. "Duty calls," she said. Then she stepped in close to Abigail, who had turned to stroke the gelding's soft, round cheek, as much to hide her own confusion as to give Laura the space to do her job. She touched Abigail lightly on the back, a feather stroke between her shoulder blades.

"There's water in the fridge in the tack room," she said. "Help yourself."

Abigail watched as Laura walked away. She wanted to kick herself—damn her stupid imagination! Obviously she had mistaken everything. Of course Laura hadn't been about to kiss her.

Laura stopped and looked back at Abigail. "Don't go," she said. "I'll only be a moment."

Abigail stared at her, wondering if she wanted to be right or wrong about Laura's intentions. She drew a shaky breath. "I...I can't," she finally said. "I have...an appointment to go to."

Laura held her gaze for a moment longer. "I'd like to see you again," she said. "Please, come by tomorrow. I'm off work, but I'll be in the office for a couple of hours in the morning." Abigail watched her walk away, wondering what she had been saying no to—and why she had lied to avoid it.

Abigail ran in the opposite direction the next morning. She had spent a restless night after her return to the hillside condo that she had rented for the week, by turns convinced that Laura's invitation to return the next day had meant nothing—and that it had meant a whole lot more. It was imagining what that "more" might be that had kept Abigail awake, her body aching and sensitive in ways and places that it hadn't been in a long time. Too long. She thought about that long-ago kiss she had almost shared with Casey and her own reaction to it. Had she really been repulsed, or had she been afraid of her own reaction, her own excitement, of half-glimpsed feelings and desires that confused her? As a young girl she'd never known anyone who was gay, and when it was mentioned by those close to her, it was always with a vague embarrassment or even outright distaste. She realized now she had always been intrigued by women who loved other women. Never enough to experiment or to risk her family's and friends' censure, though. Then she had met and married Robert, and all that had been laid to rest.

Until now. Now a stranger had stirred up all those old feelings. Now she was remembering the echoes of curiosity and urges—and yes, fantasies—that she had long suppressed.

After a lonely dinner, Abigail had taken a bath and tried to occupy her mind with the latest mystery from David Baldacci, but found she couldn't concentrate. Finally she had gone to bed, but sleep would not come. She had lain in bed, her eyes closed, and felt again Laura's hand on her shin, the gentle pressure she had exerted as she had leaned into Abigail. She remembered the warmth of Laura's body against hers and even her smell—a mixture of soap and leather and horseflesh.

She shuddered and realized her hand had made its way to her breasts. She gently stroked and pulled first one nipple and then the other. She had always had amazingly sensitive nipples— too much so at certain times of the month—and the thought of Laura's hands on them, of her mouth, lips and tongue and teeth, was almost too much to bear. She slid her hand farther down, over her belly and then farther, between her legs. A moan escaped her lips as she found her clit and began to stroke it rhythmically. Her excitement rose as she thought about Laura's hands where her own were...her mouth...

What was Laura doing at that moment? Was she lying in her own bed, thinking of Abigail and touching herself as well? That thought was enough to send the orgasm crashing over Abigail, and finally, blessedly, to usher her into sleep.

And yet now, here she was, running down the same road she had yesterday, but in the opposite direction. For once she was not lost in her music. For once her mind was absolutely clear and focused on the here and now. She stumbled to a halt and leaned forward, hands on her thighs, trying to catch her breath.

So what the hell was she doing running the opposite way?

Before she could change her mind she spun around and started running back the way she had come.

Laura looked up at a hesitant knock on her office door. Her office was small and in the back of the tack room. Here she conducted the daily business of the management of the boarding stable and riding facility. Today was her day off, but she often came in anyway, to get work done in the peace and quiet or to ride. She loved her job. It was as simple as that. And since she and Carrie had broken up six months earlier, she didn't have anything to stay at home for anyway.

Abigail stood in the doorway, a tentative smile on her face. "Hi," she said. "I hope you were serious when you said I should come by today."

Laura stared at her in silence for a moment, long enough to make Abigail wonder if her invitation had just been politeness, then she smiled widely and jumped up. "Of course I was serious! Please, come in."

Abigail allowed herself to be led into the small office. "Just give me a moment to close this program down," Laura said.

Abigail sat obediently in the chair on the opposite side of the desk. She had no idea what Laura actually did on the ranch, but she hadn't imagined a desk and computer, nor the shelving unit against the wall that was stuffed to overflowing with books. She stood suddenly and went to the bookshelf, unabashedly curious.

"I thought you said you were off work today," she said, leaning forward to peruse the titles. The shelves were filled with an eclectic mixture of fiction, poetry and nonfiction titles, many of them having to do with business administration. Most astonishing of all was that the bottom shelf was almost exclusively filled with college textbooks.

"I am," Laura said, "but I get a lot of paperwork done when no one thinks I'm around. Also, I have a paper due next week and my laptop is on the fritz at home."

Abigail turned her head to look at her. "So these textbooks—they're yours?"

Laura nodded. "Yup, every one. I just can't bear to part with them after my classes are over, especially when I've paid so much for them."

She rose and came to stand next to Abigail at the bookshelf. Abigail was acutely aware of her standing so close to her, close enough that she could feel her heat, could smell the scent of her skin and see strands of silver glinting in her hair.

"I'm sure many of them are out of date by now, though," Laura said, shaking her head. "I've been working on my MBA forever." When Abigail glanced at her in astonishment, Laura shrugged and grinned self-consciously. "I know, I know," she said. "What's a forty-seven-year-old cowgirl need with an MBA?"

"No," Abigail said, "that's not what I was thinking. I was thinking it's wonderful that you're doing it. I wish I had gone back to school."

"It's not like there's a time limit," Laura said. "You can go back any time. Look at me—I did."

Abigail shook her head and laughed softly. "I'm fifty-two—" she started to say, but Laura placed a hand on her arm. She looked fierce and determined at the same time.

"Don't say it," Laura said. "It's *never* too late."

It's never too late. Laura's words rang in her ears, reverberated through her. Abigail took a deep breath. She didn't know what might come of this, but more than anything, she wanted to find out. She ached to feel Laura's lips beneath hers, to taste her mouth, to feel her skin, to *know* her.

And herself.

She leaned forward and put her mouth against Laura's. "I hope not," she said. Her kiss was as tentative as her knock had been, and just as hopeful.

Laura tasted crisp and clean, like the mountain air. But her mouth was warm, not cool, and opened beneath Abigail's after only a moment. Something like a sigh washed over Abigail as their tongues touched. An ache curled its way up her belly, filling her with a need she hadn't known she'd been missing these last two years. Her heart pounded in her chest as Laura's tongue filled her mouth and their kiss deepened. The world felt as if it was spinning around her, and she leaned back against the bookshelf. Laura's body pressed against hers and she felt Laura's hand at the back of her neck, pulling her close. When they came up for breath a moment later, Abigail stared into Laura's gray-green eyes.

"I don't—" she began. "I mean, I've never—"

Laura placed a hand on her lips. "It's okay," she said. "All I need to know is that you want to. Are you absolutely sure you want to do this?"

* * *

Abigail hesitated, closing her eyes. As Laura watched the conflicting emotions playing over Abigail's face, she felt her own emotions welling and warring with each other. She'd had casual affairs and a one-night stand or two in her time, and enjoyed them all for what they were. She'd also been deeply in love once and had been in something close to love a couple more times. She didn't believe in love at first sight and wasn't fooling herself that this would be anything more than a vacation dalliance. But she wouldn't sport-fuck this woman. She knew now that she could not live with herself if she caused Abigail harm.

"Do you, Abigail?" she asked again. "Is this what you want?"

Abigail looked up at her. There was vulnerability in her gaze, but also a maturity and a hunger to know more, to experience whatever it was that Laura was offering.

"Yes," she said. Simply, directly, without hesitation. She kissed Laura, again, without hesitation.

Laura felt that kiss from her toes up, through her belly and right to the roots of her hair. Her pussy throbbed, and when Abigail's mouth dropped to her throat, shivers rolled over her. Abigail reached for Laura's blouse, but Laura grasped her wrists lightly and she shook her head.

A realization had hit her: it could be *her* getting hurt, rather than Abigail. No, she didn't believe in love at first sight, but she couldn't recall a time that she had been drawn so immediately to someone else. Of course it was a visceral, physical, reaction— but there was more than that. She knew that now.

"Abigail," she said, struggling to bring her careening thoughts and emotions under control. "Abigail," she began again. "I don't think I can do this."

Abigail looked by turns stunned and then deeply hurt.

"Not because I don't want to," Laura hastened to explain, taking Abigail's face in her hands. "But because I want it *too much*. I...I know this is going to sound crazy, but...I don't want to be an experiment to you. I don't want to be a vacation fling. I want...time to get to know you. And you me. I want to be the one you discover this with—god, do I! But I want to know that there is a possibility of more."

Abigail swallowed visibly.

Laura wanted to shoot herself for her clumsiness. "I'm sorry, Abigail," she said. "I didn't mean to—"

But Abigail wasn't looking hurt. She smiled shyly up at Laura. "Please, don't apologize," she said. She laughed self-consciously and shook her head. "Talk about crazy," she said. "I'll tell you about crazy." She looked into Laura's eyes and steadied her breathing. "I asked the rental agent about leasing the condo through the summer before I came over here."

At Laura's bark of laughter, she continued hurriedly, "I didn't sign the papers, but...I just wanted to know that I *could* stay longer, if I wanted to. Laura—I'd like to...take some time. To get to know each other. To get to know *myself*. I have no idea where all this will go, but...I want to explore it. With you. Not as an experiment—never that! But as my friend. As my guide. As my...lover...if you'll have me. Because if nothing else, you've shown me that it's never too late."

Laura reached and tucked Abigail's hair behind her ear.

"I'd be honored to be your guide, your friend—and your lover," she said. And then she kissed her, deeply, passionately, and without reserve. She didn't know where this might go either, and yes, she might end up hurt at the end of it. But she would accept the risk. Because, as Abigail had just said, it was never too late.

A STURBRIDGE IDYLL

Lee Lynch

The first morning of their stay, the sun poured warmth into streets that just a few days before had been wintry. Spring leapt into Sturbridge Village like a chorus line of pastel-clad dancers. A soft April rain had come in the night before on a warming wind. All of a sudden, the tips of crocuses poked up through the ground and green grass returned to the world. On the forsythia bushes were noticeable buds. Jays loudly scolded at the tops of thawed trees. Iridescent starlings rasped at one another over scraps of food. Paris felt dizzy with the balminess of noon, wondering if the goddess set the stage for them.

They rolled along a dirt path in a cart, their feet resting on hay, alone except for the driver, horses and a het couple who were way up on the front seat. It was a time to hold hands, to look into eyes, to bask in the romantic perfection of the day, to lay her head on Peg's shoulder, the world smelling of sweet warm hay. She didn't. They climbed off the cart and meandered from exhibit to exhibit. Neither of them said a word for half an hour. A bonneted woman churned butter.

"So," Paris said, afraid to break the mood, afraid not to. She tried to read Peg's eyes behind her sunglasses. "Who wore the bonnet back then? The butch or the femme?"

"Please, darlin'," Peg answered, lifting her hands as if to a bonnet. "Picture it."

"You're so true to type," she said with a laugh. "You'd look ridiculous. That doesn't mean I'd be a knockout in a bonnet."

Peg turned and measured her head, her face, with her eyes. There was such mute affection in them she wanted to be looked at like that forever. "But you would be, Paris," Peg said.

She sighed. Where was the strife with this one? When they added sex would it come? She caught herself. If—not when. They moved outside.

"I'd like two female goats when I retire," said Peg, arms folded across the top of a fence. The sheep had backed off, but a lamb bolted from its mom and returned again, curious and scared of the two-leggeds. The warm sun heightened the less pleasant barnyard smells.

"Not a couple of these wooly little things?"

"They don't stay little. And they're not very companionable when they grow up." Peg bent to stroke the wet black nose poking through the fence. "Goats are feisty and loving and funny."

Were those the qualities of a woman who could land Peg? Never mind, she told herself, she didn't want to know. The cart returned with a larger load. The horses clomped off and three families headed for the lambs, children filling the air with noise. Paris and Peg followed the cart back. A tinsmith assembled a lantern. A spinner spun sour-smelling wool with a drop spindle. A cooper up to his ankles in nose-tickling sawdust finished up a wooden bucket and handed it to them to examine. They stopped in the general store and bought penny candies. In her cavalier style, Peg offered a white bag of Boston Baked Beans.

"These could be addictive," Paris said, cracking open a handful of the sweet nutty bits.

"Never had them before?"

She looked at this real Yankee in her life and tingled again. Today, she just wanted to give in. She wanted to feel the falling in love that was going on inside her, not block it. They reached the parking lot.

She sorted through her bag and carefully set all the licorice jellybeans in the palm of Peg's hand, one by one. Peg smiled endlessly at her. The sweets, the Datsun's sweltering interior, made her sleepy. At the room, she lay on her bed and watched Peg through half-open eyes. "I hate to waste the last afternoon of vacation napping." She let her eyes close and went out like the proverbial light.

"Paris."

She was so groggy she couldn't open her eyes.

"Paris." Peg's hand firmly gripped her shoulder.

She didn't want the hand to leave. "Mmm. Peg," she said, feeling the sweet smile wash over her whole body and soul.

"You looked so peaceful, I decided to try it," Peg said. "We slept for an hour." Peg stretched and yawned, her shirt drawing tight over her chest. For once, she wasn't wearing a vest, jacket or sweater.

A current coursed along Paris's spine and goose bumps rose on her arms. Breasts, the woman had much more substantial breasts than she would have imagined. The nipples poked against her shirt like that little lamb's nose through the fence.

"We've got reservations for six P.M.," Peg said.

When Peg finished in the bathroom, Paris bent over the sink, splashing cold water on her face. She smelled Peg's minty toothpaste. She couldn't banish the sight of those breasts from her memory. Her hands hankered after their warm curves. She looked in the mirror. "The woman doesn't want you," she told herself, wishing she'd brought a lighter shade of lipstick.

There was something about applying makeup that felt like a rite of spring, and she hesitated, tremulous with fear and excitement. It was a rite she loved, even when, like this evening, it felt dangerous. Every stroke of mascara seemed to draw the night in around her like a glamorous black velvet cloak. The song "How Long Has This Been Going On" took up residence in her head. She'd brought her grandmother's tiny gold locket to go with her opal ring, and they gleamed in the mirror as she worked on her lips. She dabbed rose essence behind her ears, at the base of her neck, thought of other places. But they were running late, and that wouldn't be necessary. "The woman doesn't want you, Paris." That wasn't how it felt.

The Publick House in Sturbridge was vibrant with activity even this early in the season. The personnel all wore costumes. A young Pilgrim led them to a booth. Peg stepped behind Paris to help her off with her wool sweater.

"Oh," Paris said, surprised. She smiled her delight at Peg. "No closets tonight?"

When Peg took off her white down vest, Paris's heart stopped beating. She'd thought that never really happened until that moment. It was the Gershwin tune "Love Walked In" come to life. The tie was narrow and plum-colored and lay flat against Peg's pale yellow shirt as if she didn't have those breasts under there. But Paris knew she did, and noted how the tie lay, long and silky, exactly between them. When her heart started again it was with a thud. She wanted to stroke Peg's vest. Untie the tie with her lips and teeth. A hand in a pocket of those soft corduroy slacks, Peg was obviously waiting for her to sit first, but Paris couldn't move.

When she met Peg's eyes, she knew the clothing was no

mistake. Here was the lesbian Peg at her full sexual power, the woman who knew what she could give, willing to risk what she'd get. "You *are* Peg?" she asked aloud.

"Of course."

"How long has this been going on?" she sang, just softly enough that Peg raised one of those butchy eyebrows at her.

"Beg pardon?" Peg asked, handing her into the booth.

She sat, hoping Peg wouldn't notice the perspiration along her hairline. She couldn't *stand* their pseudo-courtship another second. What was wrong with her, with *Peg?* Was it a human trait to do exactly what one swore one wouldn't, didn't want to do? Or was it a lesbian trait, some kind of internal homophobia that ensured self-destructive behavior—or happiness?

"You're lovely in makeup," Peg said.

"You're lovely in a tie."

Peg ran her tongue thoughtfully back and forth along her bottom lip. The lines to either side of her mouth deepened. She was so incredibly good-looking. Paris had known that all along, but it hadn't entered her solar plexus before; she hadn't been this profoundly physically affected by a woman since her first lover.

Had Angela been what Peg could call butch? As seniors in high school, they'd borrowed each other's makeup, fixed each other's hair, smoked pot with college boys and caught all the arty films in Austin. They'd discovered the art galleries and scoured the newspapers for openings where they'd cop free wine and mingle with the adults, telling extravagant tales of fantastic adventures. Then they'd go parking with each other, not with the boys. Her fingers had been so eager to reach under Angela's dress and touch those drenched lips, slide up that silken canal. She could still feel Angela's hot mouth nipping at her neck.

She wanted to finger Peg's tie as she had Angela's genitals, smooth it against that valley of her breasts, slide the knot aside until she broke the plum circle, opened the butch gate, and got at the woman inside.

The wine waiter hovered. "You don't seem to be much of a drinker," Peg said.

She could taste the wine of her days with Angela. She laughed. "No. It was always superfluous."

Peg was watching her eyes, and didn't ask superfluous to what. As if measuring the moment, as if deciding for or against the distraction of wine, Peg tapped her fingers on the table. She waved the waiter away.

Almost immediately someone in a gray starched colonial-style skirt brought a basket of hot breads, sweet and yeasty-smelling. Sounds became hushed. Peg's manicured hands broke open a coarse piece of cornbread. The crumbs fell to her plate. She slid butter across the opening. Paris fondled the baking powder biscuits, pulled a hot cinnamon bun from the basket. Peg bit into her golden bread, licked her lips of butter and crumbs. Paris's roll was sticky, crunchy with bits of nuts, full of hot cinnamon and sugar. She offered Peg a bite. Peg held the cornbread out to Paris. They leaned across the table, eyes locked, and broke pieces off with their lips.

"Sweet," Paris said, closing her eyes. It tasted like the yellow afternoon.

"Sweeter," Peg said, pulling a stray nut from her lower lip with her tongue.

She ran her eyes down Peg's tie again, back up to her shining eyes, her perfect hair. Just then, she would have sold state secrets to get her hands in that hair.

Even without wine dinner got fuzzy. It seemed as if they went from bread directly to the chilly parking lot. The bakery and gift shop were open late for the weekend. Peg got them a batch of the famous peanut butter cookies. She took Peg's arm this time and huddled against her, shivering.

"Cold?" Peg asked.

She squeezed tighter against her. "No." Peg's hand encircled her upper arm.

They walked up the dark country lane that led to their motel, the white bakery box that Peg carried by its string glowing as it swung back and forth. Paris ignored the ache in her knee. This was no time for pain.

"Crickets," Peg said.

"Tree frogs," she answered.

Their footsteps were almost the only other sound. Still-leafless elm trees met over their heads, a branch creaking now and then in a breeze. She wanted the lane never to end. Peg stopped, guided her by the shoulder until they faced each other. Paris pressed her cheek to the front of Peg's cushioned vest. The top of her head met Peg's jaw. Her fingertips tingled with want.

Oh, goddess. Peg pulled her face up with two soft fingers and their mouths met, open, hot, wet, breath ragged, then met again, until Peg's hand, wide open against her back, led her forward again. They walked faster.

"What are we doing?" Peg cried, when they got inside. The blood rushing through Paris's body all but drowned out the words.

She had Peg's tie in her hands, looking her full in those commanding, desiring eyes. She pulled at the tie, stroked it and separated the two ends. Kissed the valley of Peg's breasts, spread the tie farther apart, wanting Peg's legs spread soon. She twined the tie around her hands, opened buttons. Peg stopped her, began to loosen the plum strands.

"No!" She wanted the undoing of her tie for herself. She pushed Peg to the bed, pulled off her vest, undid the buttons of her collar, pulled the shirt out from under her tie and off along with the vest. Her vision had become unfocused, but she made out Peg's breast-hugging short-sleeved undershirt. She pulled it over the tie. "Now," she said and began easing the knot down with one hand, kissing Peg's neck as she did.

"You've still got your sweater on," Peg said. "Is it scratchy?" Peg rubbed her bare breasts against the sweater and the strawberry nipples rose.

Paris brushed them with her lips as she slid the tie apart. At its tip, she freed the other end. "There," she said, "you're open." She pushed Peg, bare to the waist, down flatter on the bed and stood looking at her.

"Mmm," she said, admiring. "Who would have thought?" She hefted Peg's breasts in her hands. "So much, so soft, the cream in those Yankee pewter pitchers." She pinched the nipples, each one, with her lips. "Strawberries and cream." Peg reached for her. "No." Paris stepped back, undressed quickly, lay Peg down once more, lay on top of her, kissed her face, her neck, her shoulders, those breasts again, kissed down to her belt line.

"Paris," Peg said, trying to rise, that tender amused look in her eyes, a slight smiling curve to her lips, her hands reaching.

"Hey," Paris said, pushing her down, pushing her again, a third time, unbuckling her belt as she did, unzipping her slacks, pulling them off with her underwear. "Mmm," she crooned at the glorious sight of her and parted her legs like the two ends of her tie.

"This doesn't work for me," Peg said, her voice tight, but her telltale breathing a pant. One hand kneaded Paris's shoulder, the other had a fistful of her hair. "I need to make love to you first."

That lisp was a turn-on. "You're gorgeous," she told Peg and plunged to the knot in the tie of her legs with her mouth. "Butch," was the last thing she said before she took a faintly cinnamon mouthful of her. The word was a challenge.

THE CALL

Cheryl Dragon

I hated when FBI phone numbers showed up on my cell phone. Locking the back door to my nail salon, I debated answering. It wasn't my ex. Tess still had her own ringtone.

"Sophie's Nails."

"It's Jack." Jack was a nice middle-aged FBI agent who'd been Tess's partner for longer than the year I'd dated her. He had two ex-wives and knew what the job did to relationships.

"What's up?" Tess probably wanted the stuff she left behind and made Jack do her dirty work.

"Tess's been shot. I know you two split up, but I thought you'd want to know," he said quickly.

My stomach turned as the info processed. This was my nightmare. The very reason I couldn't be with Tess. Instead of panicking, my brain gave up control to my heart. "What hospital?"

"St. Luke's. Don't worry, it's just a—"

No time for details. "Thanks." I ended the call, jumped in my car and drove the few blocks to St. Luke's in record time.

Stalking past the admissions desk, I headed for the group of suits. Jack waved off security and pointed me to the curtain without a word. No doc or nurse could convince me Tess was okay until I saw her myself. My heart pounded as I ducked around the curtain.

Tess was attempting to sign papers with her left hand. Her slim right hand was bandaged from wrist to painted nails. Her dark brown hair done in a blunt bob was untouched by the trauma, but her face looked pale. The blood all over her clothes made my eyes well up but I forced back the tears. Obviously Tess's life wasn't in danger now. "What happened?"

"Hell. Jack, you're so dead," she said loudly. "I told him not to call you."

"Which means you knew he would and probably already had." I looked around the small area. Tess's bulletproof vest with bullets still in it spoke volumes. "You're okay?"

"I'm fine. The vest did its job. Only one sliced my hand. No broken bones." Tess's pale brown eyes searched everywhere but me.

She was still hurting, and I couldn't change my role as the bitch in the breakup. Her job meant potentially getting hurt every day, and eventually the anxiety had been too much for me. When we first met, the badge and gun had been a big turn-on. They still were, but they also meant danger. *My* biggest danger at work was nail fungus or being double-booked with clients.

The doctor stepped in before I could think of something to say.

"You're ready to go. Here are the painkiller and antibiotic prescriptions. In a few days, see your doctor to recheck that hand. When the swelling has gone down, it'll need to be rewrapped. The nurse can find you a scrub top to wear home."

Tess just nodded and took the papers as the doctor left.

Talk about trauma. The fact that Tess was only in her bra and her suit pants had gone over my head. So I wasn't a medical person—I could still see the damage. I studied Tess's torso and saw three red spots, two on her ribs and one at the edge of her breast where it peeked out of the bra.

"Did you get him?" I asked.

"Three shots to the chest. He's going to the morgue and I'm going home." Tess slid off the bed with a wince.

"Alone with that hand? No, you're not." I tugged off my thin cardigan. "Wear this."

"Soph, I don't want your pity or your sweater. This is my job and it's not going to change. I'm sorry it's hard on you, but I didn't call you. I understand you didn't want to deal with this stuff and you don't have to. I never asked you to change, but I'm not going to change, either. Because if I did, I'd resent you for it later. Do me a favor and please go. I can take care of myself."

Every word she said was true. Tess had a way of cutting through crap to the heart of every matter, and it stung. We weren't over each other. In a couple weeks, how could we be? Arguing with her served no purpose. "Nice try." I tugged the lime green sweater over her good arm and gently eased it over her bad hand. "You can't dress or undress yourself with that hand."

"Where's my purse?" She looked around and found the gray shoulder bag by her blazer. With Tess, that was as close to admitting she needed help as she got. Her sister lived an hour away, and that was her only other option.

I grabbed the blazer and tried not to look at her cut-up blouse soaked with blood. I fought the tears. Her hand had to be really messed up to bleed that much, I thought as she stood next to me ready to argue. But even if the damage to her hand was bad, she was alive.

* * *

An hour later we were in my apartment with prescriptions filled and a pizza half-eaten on the table. It felt like old times except for the nagging tension.

"We could've gotten Chinese instead." Tess fidgeted with her crust.

"Yeah, chopsticks with your left hand. That'd be a show. You need to eat before you take your pills or you'll get nauseated. Let's see if you can even open them." I nodded to the bottles.

Tess glanced at her swollen hand and then glared at me. "I don't need any pills."

"Oh no, don't do that. It's stupid to be that stubborn." I grabbed the bottle of antibiotics and set one out on the table. "Take it. The last thing you need is an infection."

A practical woman, she took the medicine. "You don't need to baby me. I know you want to be friends, Sophie, but it's too soon for me. I'm not there yet, okay?"

I looked at her, tired and hurting in my sweater, and knew we'd never manage to be just friends. One year of intense passion and now I knew I'd never *not* want her. I couldn't stop loving her no matter how much I hated her job. My resolve broke. Easing out of my chair, I straddled her lap and undid the tiny buttons to push back the sweater.

Tess looked away. "I'm not asking for random sex. My hand will be fine in a day or two. When the swelling is down, I'll be out of your hair. I appreciate the help, I do."

"This has nothing to do with your hand." I traced the darkening spots where the bullets hit her vest. "I realized something today when Jack called."

She relaxed slightly as I touched her, but didn't lean into me. Finally I gave in and kissed her softly, then pressed my forehead to hers. "Before I thought if I ever got *that* call—if you were hurt or in the hospital or worse—I'd lose it. But I didn't go all hysterical or curl up in a corner terrified like I thought I would. All those nights we were dating, I dreaded that call. But when it came, I knew exactly what I needed to do. Better yet, I did it."

Tess stared me straight in the eye for the first time that day. "You never give yourself enough credit. You're so strong, Soph."

"I grew up in the suburbs. Anyone picked on me, my big brother beat the crap out of them. This is all new for me. I love you so much, but the fear of getting that call paralyzed me every day. I can't lose you." I closed my eyes and took a deep breath before I asked the question. "Do you really still love me?"

Her answer came in a kiss as her good hand tangled in my hair. Relief jolted me as I kissed her back. We were such contrasts that somehow it worked. Tess's tight slender body had lean muscle all over while I had a curvaceous body. I pressed tightly to her and wrapped my arms around her neck.

"Is this real or am I in a coma?" she whispered.

Gently I took her injured hand and kissed the exposed fingertips. They shook and I stopped. "It's real. Please take a pain pill. You need to rest. I'll be here when you wake up."

Tess shook her head. "Having you back is all I need. Make me forget about the pain." She kissed down my neck and over my ample cleavage.

I couldn't say no to her. I never could. I needed to be naked with Tess. "In bed with you on your back and your hand propped up out of the way."

With her good hand, Tess slid under my tank top and up my back to release my bra. "In bed on my back? Since when are you so traditional?" Then she pulled the front of my tank and bra down to expose my breasts.

Her warm breath replaced the cool air and my entire body

flushed with anticipation. "Once your hand is better, we'll make up for all the lost time any way you want."

"Deal." She tongued over my nipples until I arched to her.

"Bed." I grabbed her pills and a bottle of water and set them on the nightstand in the bedroom before I pulled off my top and shimmied out of my jeans and thong.

Tess watched with a strange smile.

"What?" I demanded.

She shrugged as she stood next to the bed. "We're really back together? Just like that."

I began undressing her with impatient fingers. "Yep. You should thank Jack."

"I should've gotten shot a few weeks ago and we'd have been fine." She stepped out of her slacks and panties.

I thought about her odd take on our breakup, and it touched me. "I'd rather there was no you getting shot in this picture. You could be a lawyer or have some nice, safe desk job. We needed to be apart for me to see that's not you. Not even for me. Besides, I don't think we'd appreciate what we have with each other as much if we hadn't broken up. I've missed you so much it hurt."

I gently pushed her on her back on the bed. Putting a pillow in place, I propped her bandaged hand.

"This is very organized sex." She pinched my hip.

I wagged a French-manicured nail at her. "You behave or I'll use your own handcuffs on you. Your wrist isn't injured, so I can do it."

"Wouldn't be the first time." She kissed my hand.

"No, but this time it'll really hurt when you pull at them." I slid my knee between her legs and found her bare pussy wet and ready for me as ever. Was she wet when she saw me in the ER? In the car on the ride home? Eating pizza? We had a strong effect on each other and I knew how rare it was. How lucky we were.

She arched her back and stared at me. "Don't be a tease." Pressing my body to hers, I kissed her with a slow possessiveness, deeper and deeper as her legs tangled with mine. I kissed a path down her body, teasing both hard nipples and gently caressing each bruise. When I nipped at her hip, Tess groaned and opened her legs wide. I loved being wrapped up with her. As I tongued the perimeter of her pussy, she twisted her body from side to side.

"Behave." I held on to her thighs. Tess didn't like being passive. She normally liked to be in charge. I loved it, but I loved taking care of her too. In a week or so she'd be back to wearing a strap-on and bending me over the sofa. "Tonight I get to be on top."

Before she could think of an alternative, I curled my tongue around her clit and squeezed, swirling as her hips lifted to me. I'd missed her unique taste as much as the sound of her moans. She was primed faster than ever before, but I was right there with her.

I wasn't ready for her to come yet and slid my tongue lower into her tempting inner folds. Sucking them into my mouth, I tugged, pressing the hot flesh between my lips. Her hips pushed down and then up. I could do this all night and she'd never come. The fact that I knew exactly how to get her off made me even wetter.

"Sophie, please! Come up here. I want you."

I snaked my tongue around her clit and squeezed in time with her pulse. Then I slipped my thumb into her wet hole and fucked her. She came on me within seconds, her body shaking as she called out. I kept one eye on her injured hand, and it stayed safely on the pillow. I licked Tess's pussy until her good hand dug into my hair and pulled me up.

I trailed my tongue up her flat stomach and between her breasts until she kissed me hard. She held me tight and seemed to urge me up farther. I moved up to let her reach my breasts. Her lips and teeth showed me no mercy as she sucked and nipped. I pressed in, wanting more as I let my pussy rub her body. Tess's good hand slid down my back and squeezed my ass before dipping down to my pussy.

I shifted back and forth for attention in both spots, but I still needed more. Easing back, I ground my pussy to hers. The pressure on my clit mixed with her fingers playing inside me was exactly what I needed.

"I want to taste you, sit on my face," Tess pleaded.

"Not tonight." I groaned against her neck. There was no way to do that without risking her hand. "You need to heal."

"You're all I need." She pushed her fingers in as far as they'd go and held them.

I ground our wet pussies together and felt the pressure roll out from deep inside me. The pleasure shot through me in silent wonder. All my weight slumped onto her as my hips kept pressing. My pussy tightened on her fingers harder until my mouth found hers to kiss away my sexual daze.

Tess pulled her fingers free once my body relaxed. With a smile on her lips, she licked my cum slowly off her fingers.

"More," she said.

I kissed her and glanced at the clock. Then I shook my head. "Time for a pill." I reached over and grabbed the water and dug out a pill.

"Answer a question for me first." She sat up halfway as I sat back, still straddling her hips.

"I love you." That answered all questions for me. Having Tess back and knowing I could handle her job—even if I didn't like it.

Her finger traced my thighs. "I know. That's not the question. Remember what you asked me about six months ago?"

"Yes." Like I'd ever forget. Moving in together seemed right. Was she going to tell me she wasn't ready or that it wasn't an option? "We don't need to talk about anything tonight. Just rest."

Tess frowned. "You don't want me to move in? I understand."

"What? Wait a second. Now you want to?" Tess kept me on my toes. That much was still true.

She nodded. "Before, I thought it'd make it worse for you to have my job there in your face every day. My guns in your house permanently." Tess looked at her hurt hand. "I need you. And not just for this week with my hand. All the time. I'm not comfortable or happy without you. I've been a totally stressed-out bitch since we broke up. Just ask Jack."

"Took you long enough to realize it. I must confess that you make me feel safe. At least I'll know you're home safe with me every night." I couldn't control my smile. "Take your pill and tomorrow we'll go to your place and get some stuff."

Tess rolled her eyes but popped the pill and sipped the water. "That pill was different." She grabbed the prescription bottle and glared at me.

"Well, look at that. I brought your pain pills." I shrugged. She needed at least one night of good sleep to recover. I tugged the sheet over us as I shifted down and rested my head on her shoulder. "Now let's get some sleep."

"You'll pay for this." She wrapped her arm around me.

I kissed her throat. "I know. Tomorrow we'll get all your sex toys and sexy underwear. I'm sure you'll be very creative."

She didn't respond. I looked up to find her already asleep. I cuddled close and let her heartbeat lull me until I joined her.

THE FAN CLUB

Catherine Maiorisi

I walked into my dorm room and stumbled on a pair of black lace bikini panties lying on the floor. Dumbfounded, and completely creeped out, I turned on the light. Lace bikini panties of every color and size were draped over everything, like crepe paper decorations after a New Year celebration.

Before I could react, I was pushed into the room. The door slammed. Angry, I turned to confront my attackers. And without quite knowing how it happened, I found myself sitting in my desk chair facing seven women. Oops. I'd had a relationship with each of them, one at a time, in the last year and a half. I offered the sexy smile that got them every time, but no one smiled back. I was in trouble.

"We're here to do an intervention, Brett." It was Benita, the psychology major, who spoke.

"An intervention? Like in family therapy?"

Kate, one of the four who had her first lesbian experience with me, took over.

"We're here tonight because we love you and we believe

that continuing on your current path will destroy many lives, including yours."

"Is this some kind of joke? And why are the seven of you even together? You're not friends." I tried to stand, but Mercy of the lovely dark eyes and the seductive Spanish accent put her hands on my shoulders and pushed me down. "Stay."

"We're members of an exclusive Smith College club, the Friends of Brett Cummings. We calculate there are about twenty members," Kate continued. "But the others have graduated, so only the seven of us could be here tonight. Twenty lovers in three and a half years is impressive, Brett."

"I don't get it. I told you all up front that I don't do commitment. Did I not?"

Seven heads nodded.

"And, while I was with each of you, I never cheated. I was totally there, focused on you, loving you. We had fun. Yes?"

Seven heads nodded.

"Wasn't I honest and loving and gentle when I felt I had to break up?"

Meagan, the poet, stepped forward. She looked into my eyes. "You were all those things, Brett, and more. And that's why each of us fell in love with you despite your warnings. Then when we loved you, you left us."

"So what am I supposed to do? I feel suffocated in a committed relationship."

Benita crouched so we were on the same level. "Brett, we know your father committed suicide and you took responsibility for your younger brother and sister when your mother fell apart, so it's not surprising that you want to be free, that you're afraid of commitment. But we feel it's hurting you."

Benita stood and Kate knelt to take her place. "You are a beautiful woman, Brett, inside and outside, which is why so many of us love you. I'm grateful that it was you who brought me out. I couldn't have asked for a more loving experience. However, you're like the protagonist in that movie *Groundhog Day*, repeating the same experience over and over. By keeping everything on the surface, you're depriving yourself of love. If you continue living this way, we fear that in years to come you'll find yourself alone, never having experienced the comfort that a committed relationship can bring."

"Okay, ladies, I hear you. Thanks for caring."

"We're not finished, luvvie," Tally said, in her clipped British way.

"So when does this club of yours meet? Shouldn't I attend as the guest of honor? Maybe we can even have an orgy."

"Listen, luvvie, we know you're nervous. We think you're too focused on sex and we're very serious about this intervention. Here's our plan for your last semester at Smith." Tally put a finger up. "First, you forgo any sexual relationship until you graduate—"

"And second, I slit my wrists? Come on, ladies, get serious."

"If you approach any woman on campus, we'll take her aside and warn her to stay away. If necessary, we'll start a rumor that you have some exotic sexually transmitted disease."

"You're not serious?"

"We're totally serious." Tally held up a second finger. "Second, we want you to go into therapy to talk about this stuff. We've set up an appointment with the new psychologist. You start tomorrow afternoon."

"Now wait a minute."

"No, you wait a minute, Brett." Tally's voice was firm. "We've spent hours talking about you—"

I couldn't help the smirk. "Comparing notes, that's not fair."

"Maybe we did a bit of that in the beginning, but it was

mostly anger and a desire to hurt you that brought us together. But we're way beyond that. We all care about you. We want you to be whole, Brett, not just some fucking machine. For some reason that even we don't understand, it's important to us that you be all that you can be."

I was moved. They really cared even though I'd loved and left each of them. "I'll think about it."

"Uh-uh. Not good enough." Kate, future lawyer of America, piped up. "We've prepared a contract detailing your commitments to us." She handed me a sheet of paper. "And we're not leaving until you sign it."

The document outlined what I promised to do or, rather, not do. In truth, I'd almost come to the same conclusion as my fan club. An hour before I left for the month-long holiday break I'd ended my relationship with Mercy, and the hurt in her eyes and the sobs racking her body left me feeling guilty and ashamed. But as the month wore on, I reconsidered. After all, I was always up front about what I wanted, and learning to deal with rejection is part of life and could strengthen a person, so why should I deprive myself?

Clearly, my seven exes were serious about my not having another relationship this semester. I wasn't ready to swear off sex for that long, but signing would keep the peace. And when I found someone I was attracted to, I'd deal with the consequences. "Okay, give me a pen."

The seven women high-fived all around.

"I hear what you're saying and I appreciate where it comes from. I promise to try."

I signed. They cheered. We all hugged.

"What's with the bikini panties?"

"We wanted to get your attention, so we each contributed a couple of pairs."

"Which reminds me. Who kept a copy of my key?" I looked at Benita and Mercy, both of whom I had been involved with last semester.

Kate smiled. "We all have copies and we'll be doing spot checks to make sure you haven't brought someone here for sex."

"Okay, I get it. Now take your panties and go. My first class of the semester is tomorrow morning at eight and I need my beauty sleep."

One by one they kissed me, picked up their panties and headed for the door. Mercy was the last. Her kiss was soft and full of love.

The seven paused at the door. "Remember, we'll be watching," Kate said.

I couldn't help myself. "Please let me know when the next meeting is, I'd love to attend."

Bikini panties flew through the air, landing on my head and my lap and my shoulders. They closed the door and left. I sat there surrounded by the fragrance of them and marveled at what had just happened.

The next morning I bolted out of bed at seven forty, threw on some clothes, grabbed coffee, a banana and a muffin at the cafeteria and hustled over to the Advanced Psychology lecture hall. The professor was writing something on the blackboard when I arrived. Keeping my eyes on her back, I started up the steps, tripped and fell to my knees. Somehow I managed to keep the coffee in my hand. The class laughed. Mortified, I stood and turned to do a mea culpa, only to lock eyes with a sultry, dark-haired, dark-eyed young woman. In that instant, powerless with the intensity of her, my body in flames, it was us, only us. And I was hers forever.

She leaned in close and whispered, "Breathe."

I exhaled.

"Welcome." Her smile was blinding. She reached for the container of coffee, then sipped it. "Ah, just how I like it, black, no sugar." She took the bag from my other hand. "A corn muffin and a banana. Yummy." She turned and put everything on her desk. I stood there smirking, like a goofball.

She smiled again and waved her hand toward the chairs. "Please take a seat, Ms....?"

Somebody on the aisle poked me. I couldn't move. The person on the other side of the aisle pulled me into her chair and slid over. It was Tally. I couldn't take my eyes off the woman standing at the front of the class. This was Dr. Browning's course. Who was she? What was she doing here?

"You with the smirk on your face, please introduce yourself."

Tally elbowed me. "What's wrong with you?" she whispered. "Tell the professor your name."

Oh, my name. "Um, Cummings, Brett Cummings."

She stared right into my eyes, lifted my coffee to her lips and sipped. It was the most sensual thing I'd ever experienced. I might have had an orgasm right there if Tally hadn't pinched me. "What the fuck is wrong with you?"

"Thank you for breakfast, Brett."

Her voice was deep and strong and flowed through me like warm honey.

"So, as I was saying when Ms. Cummings interrupted to deliver my breakfast, I am Dr. Emily Caldwell. Dr. Browning was in an auto accident over the holidays and will be out for the entire semester, so you lucky devils get to study with me."

I almost swooned.

She passed out the syllabus and took care of some administrative stuff, then began to lecture. She was brilliant and pulled me in. I tapped away at my laptop, writing down as much as I could catch of the lecture. Every time I looked up, her eyes were on me. I was certain it was because she'd had the same visceral reaction as me, not because I was seated in her line of vision.

It seemed like minutes later that the class ended, but the pages of notes I'd typed assured me that the class was the usual length. I waited while my classmates spoke to her. When we were alone, I asked if I could come to her office to discuss some questions.

She took my hand and looked into my eyes. Fluttering butterflies filled me from head to toe. "No. Meet me at the Coffee Bean for breakfast tomorrow morning at eight."

Once again, I was unable to speak.

"Are you always this mute or is it me?"

I managed to croak an answer. "You."

She patted my hand. "You really need to work on that smirk and your social skills." She walked to the door. "Coffee Bean, tomorrow morning at eight." She left and I sank into the nearest chair.

Tally came back into the room. "You all right, luv? You seem strange this morning." She put a hand on my forehead. "I think you have a fever. Get some rest, but don't forget you have a therapy appointment with Dr. Caldwell this afternoon."

"Dr. Caldwell? This Dr. Caldwell?"

"Yes, this Dr. Caldwell. She's a beauty, eh? I hear she's a great therapist. Gotta run, be good."

Did the club's document apply to faculty as well as students? I jumped up. Therapists can't sleep with patients. I ran all the way to the psych building, canceled my appointment and scheduled one with another woman therapist for the following week.

The next morning I was up at six. I ran a couple of miles to calm myself, then showered, washed my hair and brushed it until it was gleaming. After changing clothes five times, I settled on skin-tight jeans and the blue silk shirt that always made me feel sexy. I strolled into the Coffee Bean exactly at eight.

My stomach lurched. Rather than one of the more private booths in the rear, she'd chosen a booth in the window, exposed to the world. I sat across from her. Had I misunderstood? For all I knew she was married. Not that that was always a problem.

We sat facing each other, eyes locked again. My body heated up, my breathing was shallow. She seemed composed but her cheeks were flushed. Maybe not a mistake.

"I'm going to order a real breakfast, and since you bought me breakfast yesterday, today is on me, Ms. Cummings."

"Please, call me Brett."

The waitress appeared and we both ordered eggs, home fries, toast and coffee.

"You had some questions, Brett?"

Questions? Oh, right, about the course. "Yes, but first, what should I call you?"

She stared out the window for a minute, then looked at me. "How about Dr. Caldwell?"

"It seems a little formal. I mean, we are having breakfast together." I flashed my sexiest smile.

"Ah, a fast mover. Well, we've just met, Brett. Besides, you're my student, so I think Dr. Caldwell is appropriate."

Her voice was so sexy. I was getting wet. I fantasized sliding under the table and—

"Why did you cancel your therapy appointment yesterday?"

Talk about throwing cold water. What now? Be honest and have her laugh or lie and be a phony?

The waitress delivered our food and we busied ourselves with buttering toast and salting and peppering eggs and potatoes. Finally, there was nothing to do but answer. I took a deep breath and raised my eyes. "Because it's unethical for a therapist to have a relationship with a patient."

"And you knew yesterday that you wanted to have a relationship with me?"

"Yes."

She nodded slowly, her face thoughtful. She reached across the table and squeezed my hand. "It's also unethical for a professor to have a relationship with a student. Can we just be friends?"

Tears of disappointment stung my eyes. Friendship when I wanted sex or was it love and commitment? My fan club would enjoy this if they knew. "Do I have a choice?"

"No. Now did you really have questions?"

"Yes. I'm looking for a job as a stockbroker. Will your psych class help me with the selling part of the job?"

"Definitely." She launched into a lecture, which I'm sure was interesting, but my mind was otherwise occupied.

When she stood to leave, I tried to nail down our next meeting. "Can we have dinner together tonight?"

"Down, girl. Remember, we're going to be friends. We are not dating. Talk to me after class tomorrow and we'll see about getting together again."

I was up and down, thinking it was going to happen, then thinking it was impossible because of her ethics. Students and professors were getting it on constantly, but I had to fall for the only ethical professor on campus. Was this punishment for all the hearts I had broken?

The next morning I arrived at seven fifty with coffee, a banana and a corn muffin for her. She showed up at eight on the dot, ignored the gifts I'd brought and went right into her lecture. A few minutes before the end of the period she ended the discussion and sat on the edge of her desk.

"I've been thinking about how best to communicate all the

material I have to cover in a way that will ensure you grasp it. So, I'll be available Monday, Wednesday and Friday mornings at the Coffee Bean for anyone with questions on what we've covered. In addition, I'll host a salon in my rooms Friday evenings for you and any of your friends interested in psychology. Each week, we'll discuss in depth what I've presented in class. Attendance at these extra sessions is optional and will not affect your grade. See you there or not." Her eyes met mine as she started gathering her things, then a student was between us asking her a question.

Anger replaced shock. I stormed out.

I moped around all day Thursday. Friday morning I stayed in bed rather than go to the Coffee Bean. By early Friday evening, I was in withdrawal but wavering about whether to go to her salon when Tally showed up.

"You want to go to the salon? Check out where the prof lives?"

It was all I needed to convince me. "You don't think it will be boring?"

"If it is, we'll disappear."

So I went. The minute I walked in, I knew it was a mistake. It was painful. She was vivacious and beautiful and I felt there was no room for me in the circle of girls surrounding her. I wandered around looking for clues to her life but found nothing. Every so often our eyes would meet across the room and I'd pretend interest in something else. After twenty minutes I was done. I told Tally I had a headache and went to retrieve my jacket and boots. When I stood after tying my boots, she was there. I swayed toward her. She stepped back.

Her dark eyes were luminous. "Leaving?"

I broke eye contact to shrug into my jacket. "I have a headache."

"We haven't had a chance to talk. Can I get you a cup of tea or an aspirin?"

I was so miserable I couldn't meet her eyes. "Thanks, I need some fresh air. Nice party. See you in class." I walked past her. Her hand gripped my wrist. "Brett."

I turned. "Yes?" I couldn't keep the hope out of my voice. "I'm sorry."

She looked pained.

"You are?" Still hopeful, I held my breath.

"About your headache."

"Thanks." I unclamped her fingers and dashed out the door.

It was freezing, a typical snowy February night, but I walked for hours, feeling betrayed and abandoned. Later, lying in bed, pride kicked in and I resolved to get over her. I would limit my contact to class.

And I did. But when Tally told me Jenna Phillips and Dr. Caldwell were an item, I was devastated.

My fan club noticed. And, worried their intervention had put me into a depression, they visited one night. They made me feel loved, something I badly needed right then. We hugged. I said I was all right, just focused on the future. But our meeting made me realize how much of my sex life was about the need for and fear of being loved. I talked to my therapist about it, but never breathed a word about her, Dr. Caldwell.

Right before spring break, just seven weeks after I fell for Dr. Caldwell, she asked me to stay after class. I hung back until everyone else had left. It was the first time we were alone since I walked out of that party. Part of me hoped she would come on to me.

"Brett, I'm worried about you. You look terrible. Do you have time for a cup of coffee before you leave?"

Up to now, I hadn't given her a chance to tell me she wasn't interested, and no way was I going to let her use the "drop the bomb and leave" move that I'd used on Mercy in December. "Sorry, I have to run." And I was out of there. Let her feel guilty for another week.

By five o'clock that night the campus was deserted except for those few with no place to go or those who, like me, chose to stay and work.

And work I did, on my thesis every day in the library, usually late into the night. I barely spoke to anyone. By two o'clock Thursday afternoon, I needed to be outside in the sunshine. I went to the dorm and changed into running clothes. I ran for miles, enjoying the snow-covered trails, letting my mind go free, feeling the warmth of the sexual fantasies about us. How could we not be together? It wasn't fair to feel so deeply attracted to someone and not be able to know her. It wasn't just sex or lust. I wanted to know her in every way, to share her life. Maybe forever.

That thought stopped me short. Forever? The fan club would be happy but the thought made me nervous, even though I wanted it with my total being. Well, I hated to break it to myself, but it wasn't going to happen. She wasn't interested.

Out of breath and approaching my favorite spot along the path, I slowed to cool down. I stopped when I reached my bench, the secret place I'd never shared with anyone. You had to walk off the path to find it. I came here often to think and enjoy the quiet and the beauty. I sat and stared at the water. Instead of batting the feelings away, I let myself experience the longing, the sadness and the loneliness. But when I felt self-pity edging in, I pulled myself together. In another seven weeks, I'd be leaving here, and her, going to New York to start my new job and the rest of my life. Dr. Emily Caldwell would still be here teaching, and after a while, she would be a distant memory.

The crunching of the snow alerted me to someone approaching. I was enjoying the solitude, so I kept my back to the path and hoped whoever it was would not try to engage in conversation. The footsteps stopped. I tensed. No one on campus knew where I was. What if it was a rapist or a killer? I slowly took my keys out of my pocket and put them in my fist with the keys sticking through my fingers like I'd learned in self-defense class.

The person moved right behind me. Whoever it was cleared her throat. Her throat. It was a woman. I relaxed somewhat and waited for her to go away, but she stood there behind me. I forced myself not to look, hoping she would get the message. Oh, hell, I was starting to get cold. I stood and turned to leave and found myself falling into those deep brown eyes. I reached for the bench to steady myself at the same time as she did. Somehow, we ended up holding hands. All thoughts of cold were gone.

"Brett, what are you doing on campus?" Her voice was accusing.

"I stayed to work on my thesis. Is that a problem?"

She shook her head. "Sorry, sorry, I was shocked to see you here. I was taking a walk and thinking about you and suddenly you were there sitting on my bench."

Thinking about me? "Your bench?"

She laughed. "I should have said my favorite bench. I come here often to think and meditate."

"Wow. This is my favorite bench. I also come here a lot."

She shivered. "I'm cold. I know you're angry with me, but can we walk back together?" She glanced down at our locked hands. "Sorry." She stuffed her hands in her pockets.

We walked in silence for a long time, a comfortable silence, then she stopped. "What am I going to do with you?"

"I have a few ideas." As soon as it came out of my mouth I

realized I sounded really piggy. "I'm sorry, that was insulting." She looked pained. "How can I make you understand, Brett? A relationship is not possible."

I opened my mouth but she put her hand on my lips to keep me from speaking. "An affair with a student could destroy my career."

I felt a stab of anger. "Really? What about Jenna Phillips? Is she exempt from these restrictions?"

She looked puzzled. "What are you talking about?"

"Don't go all innocent on me. It's all over campus that you and Jenna are a thing."

She paled. We glared at each other. I with rage in my eyes, she with...with pain in hers. I guessed it hurt to get caught in a lie.

She rubbed her temples. "Is that why you've been so angry?"

"Partly." Why not me?

"I'm not involved with Jenna." She seemed to be searching for words. "Even if she wasn't my student, I would not choose to be involved with Jenna."

"Well, she's blabbing all over the place." Na, na, I sounded like a five-year-old.

"I'll address that when classes resume next week."

So maybe Jenna was lying, but I didn't understand about us. "I'm also angry because you said you would see about us getting together again, then I find out in class that all the other students are invited. Did I misunderstand?"

She offered a sweet, sad smile. "When I thought about it, I realized it would look like we were involved." She blushed. "And I thought I would have a hard time controlling the situation if we spent too much time alone."

"Do you mean a hard time controlling me?"

"Yes." She looked into my eyes. "I've heard stories about

you, Brett. Love 'em and leave 'em stories. Twenty lovers in three and a half years. Is that right?"

I started to walk away.

"Brett, is it true?"

"Who told you?"

"I'd rather not say."

"That bitch Jenna?"

She shrugged.

"But you're different."

"That's what they all say."

"So, do I give up hope?"

Her smile was tender. "Never give up hope, Brett. None of us knows what the future holds. But we do know we can have group breakfasts and group Friday nights for the next six weeks."

"No time alone?"

"No."

She hadn't said no, hadn't said she wasn't interested or didn't love women. And at least she wasn't involved with that beast Jenna. If I focused on papers and thesis and readings, the six weeks would fly by. I nodded. "There is one thing."

"Yes?"

"Do I have to call you Professor Caldwell?"

"That's what my students call me."

"Can I hold your hand sometimes?"

"Absolutely no physical contact."

"What about phone sex?"

She blushed. "No phone sex."

"Looks like you like the idea."

"And absolutely no flirting." She bopped me on the head. "Time to go home."

In the next six weeks, I spent every minute I could with her. She made sure we were never alone. She was friendly with all her students, but I noticed Jenna only appeared in class. Sometimes, very rarely, she would touch my face or put her hand on mine, then pull back. I didn't know what to make of her breaking her own rule, but I was besotted and burning with desire and welcomed whatever crumbs she offered. If I alluded to it, she put her fingers over my mouth and shushed me. As graduation got closer, it dawned on me that we would be separated when I moved to New York City to work on Wall Street. I was frantic. She reassured me we would stay in contact.

Finally, graduation day arrived. Diploma in hand, I grinned as she made her way through the crowd to me. I was no longer her student.

She wrapped me in a hug and kissed my cheek. "I'm sorry I can't stay, Brett. I have some business to take care of. It can't wait."

I jerked back. "What?" I shouted. "You can't—"

Nearby conversations stopped. Heads turned.

She put an envelope in my hand. "I have to go." She dashed into the crowd.

She was gone. Had it all been a tease? Kate and Tally found me staring at the envelope.

Kate took the envelope out of my hand and stuffed it in my bag. "C'mon, let's go get a drink."

Good idea. I went off to get drunk with the women who loved me.

The next morning, still unable to believe it, I went by her apartment on the way to the train. She had moved out. And though I'd said rejection was part of life and could make you stronger, it hurt like hell.

The following Saturday, I emptied my pocketbook looking for a hair tie and found the envelope. I'd forced myself not to look at it, then forgotten it in the rush of the new job. I started to toss it, but I was curious. Not a graduation card. An invitation to a dinner party at eight that night at an apartment near NYU. I was enraged. Screw her and her party. Around seven fifty, I decided I needed to say "fuck you" to her face. At eight thirty, I rang the bell. The door flew open.

"Brett, I was afraid—"

"Fuc—"

Her hands cupped my face. I got lost in her eyes as she stroked my cheeks, my eyebrows, my forehead, then brushed my lips with hers. As my anger drained away, she brought my hand to her lips and kissed my palm. I gasped.

She led me to the bed. And I, always the aggressor, lay there, staring into her eyes, and let her undress and caress me with fingers gentle as feathers.

"Dr. Caldwell, the party?"

"Just us." She kissed my eyes, my nose, then my breasts. She looked up and smiled. "You can call me Emily."

"Emily." On fire, I rolled on top, pulled off her clothes and made wild, passionate, gentle, intense love to her. Good thing her loft was in an industrial building with concrete walls and floors, or for sure, we would have incinerated it that night and in the weeks following.

Turned out Em had fallen for me, too. She'd applied to New York University before we met and wanted to surprise me. She did. Three months later, I moved in with her.

My fan club was right about commitment. Em was right about never knowing what the future holds. And I was wrong about forever. Now forever doesn't seem long enough.

SEPIA SHOWERS

Andrea Dale

I don't usually bring Kathy with me when I visit my mother. Oh, my mother knows that Kathy's my friend, that we share a house. But I don't know if, when she was more lucid or now, my mother ever figured out that Kathy and I were *together*. Now, it doesn't seem worth it to try to explain. While my mother hasn't (yet) forgotten who I am, other people in her periphery have become more fluid. And although I've never exactly hidden my preferences, I don't think my mother ever fully comprehended that I'm a lesbian.

My father, god rest his soul, would never have understood. It became second nature to me not to spill the truth.

"It's time for me to go, Mom," I say. It's past time, really, but it's always hard for me to leave. I know how alone she must feel, despite the staff who check in on her several times a day, make sure she takes her pills and eats balanced meals.

It's dementia, but a mild form. She remembers me, knows the people around her. It's the day-to-day things she forgets. Where she put things. Whether she ate. Where my father, who died last year, has gotten to this time.

I know it could be far worse, but it's still hard.

I start to rise, but she doesn't let go of my hand. "I just wish you'd find someone, Dana," she says. "A good man to make you happy."

I smile for her. "I'll see what I can do."

But before I can get up, she looks over my shoulder. Her eyes widen and her free hand goes to her throat in shock. "Charlotte?" she whispers.

I turn. "Oh, Mom, it's just Kathy, here to pick me up. You remember Kathy, don't you?"

Kathy steps into the room. "Hi, Mrs. Hollander."

"Oh, Kathy, of course. Pardon my manners." My mom reaches out to take Kathy's hand. "You just reminded me of someone for a moment there."

We say our good-byes, and I gather up the box of photos she's sending home with me. In the doorway, I glance back. Mom's looking at the picture of my father on the table next to her chair.

I wish, more than anything, I could tell her that I *have* found someone, someone who makes me deliriously happy.

But I can't.

When we get home, Kathy makes tea. Lady Grey, my favorite. She knows I need to wind down. I wrap my hands around the cup as she drapes the hand-woven mohair blanket over our laps. A watery slate blue, it's the first thing we bought when we moved in together, and now it smells like roses because she'd been sitting against it earlier today.

We burrow into each other and the sofa.

I sigh, just shy of contentment. "My poor mom."

"Oh?" She's stroking my hair. I should be too old to enjoy such a simple act.

"She wants me to find a nice man who'll make me happy."

We both laugh at the irony of that. It feels good to let the sound bubble out of me, releasing the tension in my chest, an ache I didn't even realize was there until now.

"I'm sorry," I say to Kathy now. "I don't like keeping you a secret. I'm not ashamed of us, you know..."

"Oh, dearheart, I know. I've always known. And it's okay. I don't want to cause your mom distress any more than you do."

Her own parents know about us, embrace us and adore me so much that Kathy jokes if we split up, they'll keep me instead of her.

"The more important question," she continues, "is what's in the box?"

"Pictures," I say. "Uncle Dan's been reorganizing the storage unit and brought them to her, and she thought I'd like to go through them. I'll scan them, and hopefully get some stories out of her before..."

I can't say the words "before it's too late," but Kathy knows. She kisses my head, my cheek, and I take a few shuddery breaths to center myself.

Later that night, when I most want to sleep, most want to run away from the thoughts, I lie awake.

When Kathy rolls over and spoons against me, her back to my front, I snake my hand beneath her arm and grope for her hand. In her sleep, she twines her fingers with mine.

It's all I can do not to squeeze so hard I wake her.

How can it be possible to forget?

I don't want to forget.

I press my face into her shoulder. The soft strands of her hair tickle my face. Disengaging my hand, I gently run it across her hip, savoring the spot at the joint that's warmer than the rest of her, then down her thigh. She's taken up running again in an effort to stave off the middle-age spread, and even with my light touch I can feel the muscles, hard and strong.

I hadn't been thinking about sex, really, I hadn't, but apparently my exploring hand plants the idea in Kathy's subconscious. Still asleep, she murmurs, a happy hum of a sound, and presses herself back against me.

I vow never to forget the feeling of her body against mine, nor how my own body responds to it. My nipples harden, pressing against her smooth back. Even in the dark, I know the constellation of freckles on her shoulders, and I trace them with my lips and tongue, still gently, easing her into wakefulness. At the same time, I snake my hand back up to circle her nipples with my fingertips, feeling them crinkle in response.

When she does finally rouse, she's already half-aroused; I can smell her earthy musk. I move my hand to touch her, but she captures my wrist.

"No," she whispers. "Let me."

I assume she means she'll pleasure herself—although, half-lust-fogged myself, I'm not sure why—but instead she rolls over, insinuating one of those strong thighs between mine, pressing against my mound. Almost involuntarily, I grind against her, smearing her skin with my own wetness.

I hadn't realized how excited I'd become, either.

She cups my face, then tangles her fingers in my hair, pulling me in for a kiss that starts sweet but rapidly grows urgent. Now I feel almost frantic, not for orgasm, but to kiss her, feel her lips and teeth and tongue. To lose myself in the sensation and forget my sadness.

But not forget her, not forget how she feels, how she makes me feel. Never that.

She rolls me on my back, rises above me, her thigh flexing against me as she takes first one, then the other nipple in her mouth. We're past the soft strokes like the ones I used to wake her. Now she's nipping, pinching, tweaking.

I'm ramping up, passion overtaking rational thought, and yet the two are fighting against each other. I want to track every sensation—her flesh against mine, her quick breaths, the taste of that drop of sweat I just kissed off her forehead—create snapshot memories, preserve them.

But then she begs, "Come on, baby. Come for me." Her voice is tight, and I know she's on the verge, too, from the way I've been humping up against her in my own quest for orgasm.

"You...first..."

"No." It's a moan. "You."

I'm not sure which one of us starts first, just that one triggers the other, and back again, and again. We build on each other's joy, a twining spiral of fever pitch and release.

"I love you," she whispers, and I'm sure I will always remember that sound, and the catch in my own throat as I say it back to her.

Now, exhausted, I finally sleep.

I'm busy the next few days, so it's a while before I have the chance to look through the box of photos. I curl up on the sofa with another cup of tea. Kathy's already there, feet propped up, laptop keys clicking as she works.

She puts down the computer and sets her glasses on her nose. They're from the dollar store, shocking green, and she wears them on a beaded chain she made. I don't need reading glasses—yet—but I borrow them a couple of times to look at some of the older photos where the faces are small and a little blurred.

Then I pull out one, and in my own intake of breath I can hear the echo of my mother's gasp from the other day, when she saw Kathy.

Kathy plucks the photo out of my hand. Her eyes widen.

"Yeah," I say. "So, are you a vampire or a time-traveling alien?"

The picture is of my mom, I'm guessing during college from her age and clothes. The black-and-white photo shows her with another young woman, their arms around each other's waists as they laugh into the camera. My mom's scarf is whipping in the wind, while the other woman has a hand up to keep her own hat from blowing away.

The other woman looks a hell of a lot like Kathy.

Kathy flips the picture over. "Betsy and Charlotte," she deciphers the faded penciled words. "Who was Charlotte?"

"I have no idea." I dig into the box. "I don't remember Mom ever mentioning her."

There are more photos of Charlotte, more than I've seen of any other friends of my mom from that era. The ones she'd been close to, she was still in contact with (if they were still alive)...or so I'd thought. The more we find, the more we realize Kathy isn't Charlotte's doppelgänger, but at the right angles, there's certainly a resemblance.

And, I suspect, there had been something going on between my mother and the lovely Charlotte.

"Tell me if I'm losing my mind..." I begin.

"Always," Kathy vows. I smack her thigh, which reminds me of a few nights ago, which distracts me for a moment.

"There's something about the way Charlotte is looking at the camera in some of these," I finally say. "And the way my mom and Charlotte are together. I know women were...they held hands as friends more often then, that sort of thing. But I feel like I'm seeing a...closer relationship?"

"I was actually thinking the same thing," Kathy agrees. "These shots here, of the two of them"—she fans them out on the coffee table—"I think they might have been done with a self-timer, rather than someone else taking the picture."

"Which might explain why they were free to be so... snuggly."

"I think," Kathy says with a grin, "that your mother might have some 'splaining to do."

By the time I visit my mother the next day after work, I've convinced myself I've been reading too much into the pictures.

We have our usual hellos, the small talk about the food at the home, that she won at bingo yesterday. Then I bring out the manila envelope.

"I started scanning those pictures you gave me," I say. She doesn't remember, so I remind her about Uncle Dan bringing them. I'm not sure if she agrees because I jog her memory or because she doesn't want to admit she's forgotten—whether to me or herself isn't clear. Is that what we fall into? Playing games with ourselves, convincing ourselves everything is okay?

"I was wondering," I continue, handing her a photo. "Who's Charlotte? I don't think you've ever mentioned her before."

I watch as an array of emotions cross my mother's face. I'm not imagining things. I see fondness, sadness...love.

"She was a friend," my mom says.

"From the looks of it, she was more than a friend," I say.

She glances at me. I raise my eyebrows, but I also smile. "Mom," I say gently. "You can tell me."

She bites her lip, and tears fill her eyes. She doesn't cry, though—she's cried in front of me only once before, and that was when my father died. Our family, we don't believe in that sort of thing. Thankfully Kathy's broken me of that bad habit. And then my mother tells me the story. Not in graphic terms. In fact, she dances and skirts around things, darting looks at me to see if I'm picking up the innuendo. Then she looks away again, lost in a memory that thankfully she still has, still clings to.

What comes out is roughly what I'd suspected. A college fling, she says, that nobody else knew about. It was more than that, though, I can tell from her voice that she'd loved Charlotte. She tells me she and Charlotte had a relationship, but it wasn't as accepted back then, and—as she insists over and over—she loved my father very much. I'm tempted to say, "So you're bisexual—that's fantastic," but I think using the word will shut her down.

So I give her my support, my understanding. She seems to relax when she realizes I'm not judging or questioning her.

Ever since I saw the photos of her and Charlotte and guessed what might have happened, I'd been thinking. My mother may have dementia, but she hasn't forgotten everything. I can't treat her like a child.

She wants me to be happy. She deserves to know I am.

I tell her about Kathy.

My mother is silent for a long while. A heavy knot forms in my stomach. Was this a mistake?

Then, finally, she asks, "Are you happy?"

"Happier than I ever could have imagined," I tell her. "She's the one, Mom. I'm going to spend the rest of my life with her."

"It won't be easy," she says. She always has to warn me of the negative side of things.

"We've been together for eleven years," I say. "We've weathered the negative so far."

"Well, then," my mother says. "Well. What I want to know

is, when's the wedding? When do I get to walk you down the aisle?"

I laugh, and we cry, and then we talk about wedding dresses.

We have the ceremony in the courtyard of the care facility. Just family and a few close friends. The water splashing in the fountain sparkles in the sunlight, and the colors in the tiles are mirrored in the riotously blooming flowers.

On our wedding night, kissing Kathy is like kissing her for the first time and the millionth time, new and yet familiar, fresh and yet filled with the memories of every kiss we've shared.

Before I fall into the mindless spiral of desire, though, I realize something.

What's important isn't the future, isn't the possible forgetting. What's important is right now, this moment, glorying in everything that it is with no other goal than mutual pleasure.

Someday, down the line, we might forget the person...but we can never forget the love.

FAITH

Jean Roberta

Every time she opens the door, I'm reminded of a sunrise. Or maybe a moonrise, a less flashy and more mysterious form of illumination.

Her name on paper is Leah Wagoner, which suggests gypsies on the move. She has deep brown eyes, glossy dark hair that shows bronze undertones in afternoon sunlight. Her hair flows over her assertive shoulders when she doesn't tie it back. Her breasts are full and joyful. She wears knit tops in bright colors that present her cleavage like an inviting valley in an ad for travel or real estate. The way she stands in her doorway suggests that her legs and feet would rather be dancing. Or walking away.

She gets mail from left-leaning political organizations that want her to sign petitions against human rights abuses, from foundations that want her to help save the whales, the dolphins, the wild birds, the land, the water, the forests and to join the fight against breast cancer, birth defects, diseases of the heart, lungs, liver, pancreas and brain, as well as malnutrition and a shortage of artificial limbs. She subscribes to a magazine about graffiti around the world—who knew that "Fuck Off" in a bouquet of languages could be a subject of art criticism? She also gets letters from New York City, hand-addressed by a Matthew Wheeler. His wheels don't seem to bring him here.

"I got your mail again." *Including a message from your male.* I smile, not knowing whether this is the most appropriate expression to accompany my offering. Should I seem happy that local mail delivery is so careless? Should I wince sympathetically and run the risk of looking self-indulgent or bitchy?

"Thank you. It's very nice of you to bring it over, Cass." She barely glances at the bundle I brought her before throwing it onto a small table in the entranceway.

She knows my name, though I don't remember introducing myself. My memory must be slipping.

"No problem," I tell her. I know I'm blushing like a teenager. "Your house is right on my way." Duh. Every house is on the way to somewhere.

Why is her mail so often delivered to my house, and never mine to hers? Or does she have a stack of envelopes for me, yellowing in a kitchen drawer? Or thrown out with the garbage? It would be rude to ask.

She has more to say. "It must be part of the grand plan. They say nothing happens by accident."

Is Leah inviting me to become a casual friend, someone she can joke with about Matthew? (*"Men!"*) That wouldn't work, at least for me.

I have never felt so moved by the curves and indentations of another female body. The creases of her elbows tell their own stories. The dark moisture at her armpits looks as rich as the juice of a just-ripe fruit. Her denim-covered crotch sends strong, slow vibrations in my direction. I love the way her hips rock slightly as she shifts from foot to foot. Her smooth neck shows innocence while her voice suggests experience.

If nothing happens by accident, my stupid crush must be a side effect of a mail carrier's dyslexia, a little joke of the goddess. I couldn't really have a crush on someone I hardly know. I must be projecting all sorts of desires onto her because I've been so disappointed by the women I know too well. Plus I'm starving for skin and pussy. I need to stop this.

"I'll see you next time—" I tell her, already turning away.

She pulls me to her with one arm around my shoulders and the other around my waist. Her naughty eyes look into mine as she closes my mouth with a soft kiss. I can't breathe.

She grins. "Sorry if I guessed wrong. But I don't think I did."

"You're joking." It's all I can think of to say.

"I'm checking you out. I'm glad you're still here."

I'm still standing in her doorway, in full view of the street. She doesn't seem to care, but I don't want either of us to be driven out of this neighborhood by a mob of peasants with torches and pitchforks. I'm not sure the town we live in has completely forgotten its rural roots.

On the other hand, her interest in me is a miracle. She only wants to fool around, but that's so much more than I thought I'd get. I should accept it and be grateful.

"Leah—"

"You never noticed me before, but fate brought you to my door. You need to have faith in the process, babe."

I step in and close her front door behind me, feeling as if I've crossed a line. I laugh on an exhale. "Come here." I pull her to me. Her breath is in my face, and I can feel the heat of her scalp. I press my lips to hers. She responds like the hot bitch she is, opening her lips for my tongue. I taste her and swallow her moan.

She catches her breath. "Cass, you're so thin, always on your feet. You need another kind of exercise." She grabs one of my hands and leads me into her front room.

I haven't studied her décor, but she obviously has faith in her own taste. Her walls are a womblike dull red, her carpet is pearl gray, her wooden furniture looks old and well cared for. The house is small, but she has created interesting effects in every inch of space.

She doesn't want us to stop here. She leads me through the kitchen to a bedroom in the back of the house. The walls are covered with paintings of trees, houses, back lanes, skies and a few people.

Now I know where I heard her name before. She's the artist who made a painting of the public library to be hung inside it. For a day, this news pushed all the world's wars off the front page of the newspaper.

"Look at this." She shows me a big canvas, propped against the far wall.

It reminds me of a picture in an elementary-school reader. It shows a street full of people going about their business in dazzling sunlight. Three-story vintage houses are interspersed with modest bungalows, some painted in quirky colors like salmon or mint green. Flowers in neat rows can be glimpsed in the background. A young girl is pulled down the street by a dog, a frisky terrier on a leash. A small adult holding a comically high stack of white boxes rushes away from a parked van with the name of a business on its side.

Holy sesame oil. The sign on the van reads "Ambrosia Catering." It's my business. And the busy caterer who seems totally unaware of how she looks could only be me.

"You painted this?" What I really want to know is why.

"Do you like it? City Council commissioned it for the

centennial." So this is how I'm going to be remembered in times to come. But it's not about me.

I must be diplomatic. "It's true to life. Well not really, but you've captured that whole block."

She seems to be keeping a laugh bottled up like an unpredictable genie. "If that's all you have to say, let me show you my bedroom." She presses against me from behind, holding me possessively.

I pull her hands off my sweaty rib cage and turn around to face her. "Why am I in that painting?"

"Why not? You're one of the local landmarks." But her picture doesn't show me running a business. It shows the business running me.

Even still, I want her. As it happens, I can spare the afternoon.

She leads the way to her bedroom, which is dominated by a high double bed covered with a thick purple duvet and a row of gold velvet pillows with tassels that look suitable for tickling nipples.

Before we can climb onto her love-nest, I press her against the wall. "Stalker," I growl into her ear. I hope I sound sexy.

"You're hard to ignore. You're so much bigger than your size."

I like this better than the usual question about why I'm not fat if I'm really a cook.

She wraps her arms around me as I hold her head in place so I can kiss her the way she deserves. We melt together as our tongues touch. I slide my hands down her sides, feeling her hot flesh through her clothes. I unbutton her cotton shirt, exposing her collarbone and her smooth, creamy skin an inch at a time. As soon as her shirt opens, she sheds it in one fluid motion and slides down the zipper of her jeans.

Leah was born to display herself. She tosses her flowing hair over one shoulder as she reaches behind herself to unhook her shiny black bra and fling it onto a chair. She bends forward to push her jeans and panties down her legs, keeping one eye on me as she steps out of each leg.

"Baby." I wrap my arms around her and approach one of her puckered nipples with my mouth.

She pushes me back with a hand on my forehead. "No clothes. I want to see you too."

I pull my sweater over my head with both arms, and she takes it away to throw it over her own clothes. My underwear is utilitarian white cotton, so I quickly take off my bra and pull my panties down with my corduroy pants, not wanting her to think I lack flair.

We fling ourselves onto her bed like children. I maneuver her onto her back, spread her like a starfish and admire the view for a moment. Her body is a landscape that I would like to explore for as long as she lets me. Or until she gets an important long-distance call.

Her nipples have a purplish tinge, and they are both hard, wanting attention. I fasten my mouth on one and suck it steadily, pulling it carefully between my teeth. I hear her faint hiss as I flick my tongue across the swollen bud, kneading her breast. I move to the other one and repeat the process, stretching each nipple to match. I reach for a pillow, find a tassel and use it to brush her tormented nipples as though painting them. She squirms and laughs.

I kiss my way down her breastbone, past her waist and her touchy, gurgling belly. She strokes my short hair, urging me on. I reach her dark, curly bush and notice the moisture sparkling on the ends of her hair.

"Ohh," I moan. "I could just eat you up, honey."

"You're the food expert." She is shamelessly offering herself to me, and I am amazed at my luck.

I part her lower lips and sink a curious tongue into her slit. I taste salt and musk and feel her hips move. Holding her womanly asscheeks with both hands, I find her clit and tease it with the tip of my tongue. I suck it into my mouth, feeling her quivering tension.

She is so responsive that I'm tempted to keep her trembling on the brink for as long as possible, but I don't want to wait.

I slide one finger into her hot, wet center and feel pebbled flesh like the stones of a riverbed. I rub and stroke, feeling her move shyly at first. Her hips push forward, pushing for more, and I match her rhythm until we are pumping together. By now I have three fingers buried in her. The squishing sound seems to fill the room.

Leah hisses in my ear. She's so close, and I want to give her everything she needs. Did she whisper my name?

Come, come, come, I chant silently. She seems to hear me, and her breath grows louder. "Ahh-ohh." Her clit is so swollen now that it couldn't hide from me if it wanted to. I settle my lips around it and lick.

As I expected, she comes loudly. I'm glad she doesn't try to control the volume. I feel a spurt under my fingers as though a fountain wants to burst out of her. The bedspread under us is soaked. I try to feel relieved that I don't need to know how to clean it. I don't live here.

I hold her head against my upper chest, rocking her gently. "You're such a woman, Leah. How long has it been?"

"Too long." She laughs without bitterness. "Worth the wait, though. How long for you, babe?"

I count the months. "Almost a year now. It wasn't simple. When I caught my partner with my friend, I told her to leave.

She finally moved out, but she wanted a share of the business. I can tell you all about it, but not now. Please not now. I don't want to ruin the moment."

"It's okay, Cass." I can feel her breathing. "Is that a nickname?" She runs a hand through my hair, making me shiver.

"Short for Cassandra, the woman who could always predict bad times, but no one believed her. Thank my hippie parents."

She sighs, snuggling closer. "My parents were the opposite. Straitlaced." I can feel her voice in my flesh as well as hear it. I wonder if I could come just from the sound waves. "My brother and I were into art and music and late nights, but they wanted us to be business tycoons. Or at least corporate lawyers. Matt changed his name and moved to New York to seek his fortune."

"Your brother?"

"Yes. He plays trumpet for Run Like Hell."

I'm embarrassed by my ignorance, but I can't pretend to be impressed by a band I never heard of.

It's her turn to comfort me, and she traces circles around my nipples, turning them into stones. "It's okay if you don't know the East Coast music scene, Cass."

I want to hear every kind of music that turns her on, but not yet. Neither of us wants to keep talking.

She shifts, pushing me effortlessly underneath her warm curves. "I want to have you, honey. Will you take my cock?"

My cunt answers for me, clenching in response. My bones have turned to rubber and hot lava runs from my heart to my crotch. I don't want to want this dangerous invasion, but I do. "Mmm."

She positions me on all fours on her bed, where I balance in twitching anticipation while she pulls something out of a bedside table. I turn my head to look, and she slaps my behind, making me jerk. I hear her fastening a harness around her hips and I see something long and smooth bobbing in front of her. She uses one hand to rub something on it, and I know how easily her tool will fill me.

And then she is kneeling behind me, guiding it into my grateful opening. *Yes!* I can't help breathing in rhythm, then groaning.

"Good girl. You like that, don't you?" It's beyond my expectations.

She pushes forward and I push back. It feels as if we're going somewhere, like rowers or railroad workers, laying new track. She reaches beneath me to find my clit and roll it between her fingers.

I shatter into particles of colored light, howling to the ceiling. She presses deep into me, as though she wants us to be joined forever. That's a grotesque thought, but I love it in the moment.

She gently withdraws from me, and the movement brings our combined smells to my nose. Nothing beats the earthy musk of women together.

Leah's cock goes back into the drawer where it lives, and Leah curls up behind me, spooning me against her. We sigh in unison.

"I didn't offer you a drink." She sounds apologetic. "Would you like a screwdriver?"

I laugh. "I won't say no." Now I know that she's not finished with me. We're just resting between rounds.

We walk to the kitchen, comfortably nude. My skin feels moist all over, as though I am a fresh fruit, full of juice. Leah pulls orange juice out of the fridge and a clear glass bottle out of a cupboard. She pours with a calm hand and hands me a drink.

We sit in her front room, sipping drinks. I run my cold glass over each of her assertive breasts, making her squeal. She grabs my arm and does the same to me.

Pausing for breath, she looks at me thoughtfully. "I hope you can forgive me, girl."

"Psh. Nothing to worry about, Leah. It was totally consensual."

Her look alarms me. "You don't know what I mean. I opened your mail."

The lightning in my belly tells me exactly what she opened. It's from Kelly or her lawyer. It's a piece of the puzzle that I should have known about before I offered to buy her out to get it over with. I no longer want to be kept in the dark about anything. "I'm not blaming you, but I need to see it."

Leah stands up and goes to an oak sideboard that looks as if it has held a few family secrets in its time, such as Uncle Ned's hip flask from the 1920s. So that's where my misaddressed mail has been kept.

She brings me four envelopes, each neatly slit open with a knife. There is an ad for real estate in a treeless, overpriced new neighborhood, a religious tract about the End of Days, an ad for a sale on cookware that ended three months ago. Then there is the letter with my name on it in familiar handwriting. It is addressed to my house, formerly our house. There is no good reason why it wasn't delivered to me on time.

"I opened it before I realized what it was." She is twisting her hands. "Then I didn't see how I could give it to you. Sorry."

I unfold the single sheet of paper and see the angry words running down at a left-to-right slant. This toxic spill was not written by a rational adult. I read "never listened to me," "too busy taking care of yourself" and "one-sided relationship." Her last childish rant still had the power to hurt.

Leah wants me to understand her motives. "I didn't know all the circumstances, but I didn't want you to see that. I know I was wrong, but I couldn't put that in your hands."

I could choose to believe in the deceptive nature of most dykes, or most people. I could confront her about manipulating me, just like my ex. Or I could choose to believe her intentions were good enough. Faith would make the difference.

I look into Leah's dark-chocolate eyes. "Forget her. You didn't need to read that either." I stuff each letter back in its envelope and tear each one into even strips, making sure I won't leave any legible pieces. "Now it needs to go where it belongs. In the circular file." I hold out my fist and Leah opens her palm to receive the scraps of paper.

She struggles to control a grin as she walks to a wicker basket in the corner and lets the paper flutter in like dead leaves falling from a tree.

"Done." I reach out to touch her.

"Done." She reaches down and pulls me to my feet. "Now let's go back to bed and finish what we started."

"Then complain to the post office."

"I'll leave that to you." She wraps her fierce arms around me and lifts me off my feet. My complaints can wait.

RISKING IT ALL

Lynette Mae

My shift finally ended. I turned the corner onto our street, exhausted, sweaty and numb from hours of stress. It was the kind of night that tests the mettle of everyone who has ever donned a uniform and balanced duty and devotion for the public good. That's not to say cops are saints, and I know we're far from perfect, but I'd like to think that it's true what they say about law enforcement. It's a calling.

It had been a night like no other. I've taken more risks than I can count over the years, chased criminals at hair-raising speed, run toward gunfire rather than away and engaged the evils of humanity without much thought. But on this night I'd been tested professionally and personally in ways I could not have imagined before. My emotions were pushed to the breaking point. Thankfully, it was over now. But it wouldn't really be over until we were both home.

The last time I talked to you was when the radio call came in. We had just finished having dinner together, a treat we rarely allow ourselves because you always say people will talk. I say, "Screw them," and you just shake your head at me. We leaned against the bumpers of our cars and recited our normal give and take.

"I love you."

"More." You smiled that special smile that never fails to set my heart tripping in my chest.

Suddenly, the horrific transmission silenced our playful banter. A bloodcurdling scream from the police radio raised every hair on my body. "Oscar Four! I've been shot!"

Every nerve ending sprang to high alert as voices demanded his location. We jumped into our cars, instinctively heading toward the east end of town, where the Oscar squad worked. You peeled out of the lot just ahead of me, your hand out the window making the *I love you* sign. And then instead of lovers we were two cops, lights flashing and sirens blaring through the city. In the next seconds, responding officers' excited chatter and supervisors shouting for an ambulance mixed with the sounds of the wounded officer's cries over the radio. We pushed our vehicles to the limits, screaming through the streets heedless of our own safety. This was different. One of *us* was down. We needed no official declaration. The manhunt was on.

A minute and a half later we arrived in the area. EMS administered first aid to the injured officer and a ring of uniforms surrounded the scene. The rest of us began to scour the surrounding area for the suspect: a white male last seen driving an older-model Ford truck, orange with a white stripe down the side. "That thing should stick out like a whore in church," I told the cop on scene who gave us the description. I only hoped the bad guy hadn't been able to reach the interstate. I wanted to catch him and I wanted to catch him now.

We fanned out across the sector with our fellow officers,

each with our private thoughts for our fallen comrade as we searched. Every cop in the city was in this zone. This guy had to turn up. The helicopter was in the air, checking beyond the immediate grid, just in case he'd gotten farther than we'd anticipated. We were updated regularly with tips and possible sightings, but nothing seemed to be panning out as the hours dragged on. The wounded officer was holding on, and his strength bolstered our resolve.

Finally, around two A.M. a gas station clerk called to say a truck matching the description had just pulled in behind his business. I was four blocks away. I stood on the accelerator and wished for a rocket booster that would get me there faster. My approach was from the west and I immediately saw the rear quarter panel of the truck as I made the corner past the building. Orange paint sent adrenaline surging through my veins. This is the moment cops dream of. With no time to think about anything but preventing escape, I swung my car around to block the suspect vehicle. Another squad car entered the parking lot from the east and we drove our bumpers simultaneously into our target, pinning it there.

I hit the release button on my assault rifle as I threw open the door and launched from my driver's seat toward the car, leading with my muzzle. I moved swiftly to a position just behind the driver's door. In my peripheral vision I could see the other officer approaching the passenger side. The suspect leaned across the bench seat in that direction. Tunnel vision took over, my focus like a laser beam on the driver. The suspect's right arm came up.

"Gun!" the other officer shouted. The world around me exploded in gunfire and flying glass. The popping sound of a pistol and the discharge of my rifle seemed to happen in slow motion. I swear I could see the spent casings ejecting from the port. I fired three times. The suspect jerked each time our bullets struck him. When the firing stopped, my ears were ringing. I was standing at the driver's window looking at the suspect sprawled inside the cab, his right arm outstretched and a pistol just beyond it on the seat. Shards of glass covered everything, including me. I raised my eyes, looking across the interior to where the second officer stood.

"Dana?"

"Holy shit!" I breathed.

You were standing there much as I was, glass clinging to your hair and clothes, tiny cuts on your face and arms. I gulped audibly just before a wave of nausea rolled through my gut, and tried not to think about how this might have turned out. The stunned expression on your face said you were having the same thoughts about me. Neither of us moved. We just blinked and stared. I saw the love in your eyes, but it was fear beneath the surface that twisted my heart. I opened my mouth to speak and nothing came out. The gravity of what had nearly happened overwhelmed me. What if... I cut my eyes to the ground, unable to cope. Service and sacrifice had taken on a whole new dimension.

A flood of officers descended on the location, and controlled chaos erupted around us as the parking lot became posted as a crime scene. Yellow police tape cordoned off the area, investigators swarmed, flashbulbs popped and bullet casings were marked on the blacktop. Each of us was whisked away in a different direction, sequestered pending questioning by detectives and union reps. At headquarters, every once in a while I'd catch a glimpse of you as we moved through different stages of the process. I knew rationally that policy and protocol required us to be separated, but I wanted to see you.

No. I wanted to hold you.

Sometime in those next hours you left a message on my cell that you took a few stitches, but were fine. "See ya later," you started to end, with your standard cheerfulness, and I pictured your dazzling trademark smile. Then I heard you pull in a shaking breath. "I love you, Dana." I closed my eyes and absorbed the tenderness in your voice. Even in the direst of circumstances you give me what I need, and I'm certain I'm not deserving.

At nearly four A.M. I pulled into the drive, longing for the sanctuary of home, our comfortable bed and you. I stripped off my uniform as I moved deliberately through the shadows of the house. The release of the Velcro on my duty belt and the straps on the body armor made sharp noises in the otherwise still darkness, while the chill of the air-conditioning began to ease the fire beneath my skin. Once the layers of work attire and finally my underwear had been shed, I walked nude across the living room, slid open the patio door and stepped onto the lanai. The night air was still thick, hot and sticky.

I silently descended the three stairs into the pool and submerged myself in the crystal water. Cool, liquid relief suffused my overheated body. The light from the full moon overhead and the soft glow of the garden lighting beyond the screen enclosure were the only illumination in the otherwise dark backyard. I dipped under, pushed off from the side wall and crossed the length underwater to surface at the other end. The chill of the water penetrated my body's core, exhilarating and soothing at once. I turned onto my back and floated weightlessly, allowing the peaceful comfort of home to ease the insanity of our shift. I completed another noiseless lap, reveling in the sensation of the water flowing over every inch of my skin. The water muffled all sound to wrap me in fluid quiet, suspending me in its alternate peaceful reality.

I popped up in the shadows at the far end of the pool, suddenly aware of eyes on me. My gaze tracked toward the patio doors to find you standing on the threshold, silhouetted in the light from the house, watching me in the water. Our eyes met across the humid night. A knot of desire twisted in my stomach as you stepped onto the deck, your face intensely focused, staring. Your lips turned up into a soft, sultry smile, a mixture of gratitude and hunger. I opened my mouth to ask you how you were, but the smoldering look in your eyes stole the air from my lungs and the words died on my lips.

Wordlessly, you dropped your gun belt and removed your outer uniform shirt, ballistic vest and T-shirt, exposing your high, firm breasts and sleek torso in the moonlight. My breath caught in my chest. Heaviness in the pit of my stomach quickly spread between my legs, making it difficult to tread water. I crossed to the built-in seat along the wall in the deep end of the pool, bringing me closer to the side, closer to where you stood in just your BDU pants and boots.

When you bent over to untie your boots, your breasts swayed slightly as you worked the laces free. I felt light-headed. You kicked off the boots and socks, unfastened your belt. I stared as you slid your pants down over your hips to your ankles and stepped free. My breathing came faster now as I took in every inch of your well-muscled, beautiful form. Wetness seeped between my legs that had nothing to do with the water in the pool, and my nipples tightened with desire at the sight of you standing before me so beautiful and proud in the moonlight.

You smiled knowingly and eased into the water beside me, settling on the step. I took your hand to pull you onto my lap. Your legs snaked around my waist and I reached out to grab your ass and nestled you tightly against my stomach.

A bandage covered the area on your forehead just above your left eyebrow. I touched a finger tentatively just at the edge of the gauze. "Can I see?" You nodded and I carefully lifted the tape and the bandage, revealing a line of sutures beneath.

"Sorry." I lightly touched my lips to the wound, then replaced the dressing. I tilted my head to search your face and saw the fear from earlier that stopped me abruptly. We locked eyes, sharing a nonverbal connection for long moments. I could almost hear the sounds of the guns and the breaking glass vibrating between us. "Do you want to talk about it?" I finally asked. The silence stretched for so long that I wondered if you'd heard me. After a while you tightened your hold and shifted more securely in my lap. Tears welled in your eyes. "Baby, it's okay," I whispered against your skin.

"He reached for the gun. All I could see was his hand reaching for it. I—I didn't see you...." A single tear tracked down your face. I brushed it away with my thumb. For the first time I realized that you were experiencing the same fear for me. My heart broke watching the raw agony that played across your features. I had no idea what to say because I was just as traumatized by the events. We'd stared down a cop shooter, responded with force and killed a man, risking everything. *Everything.* The memory of your stricken face mirroring my panic drove the danger frighteningly home. The peril of loving another cop made crystal clear.

But we survived. You trembled against me. I wrapped my arms tightly around your neck and buried my face in your hair, drawing comfort from the feel and the scent of you. "It's okay," I whispered. "I'm okay. We both are. Shh..." I threaded my fingers though your dark hair and placed feather-light kisses along your shoulder, up your neck to your face. "I'm here, Mandy." Our lips met softly. You kept your eyes open as if to reassure yourself that it was the truth. Your hazel eyes change color like a mood ring, always allowing me to read your emotions and needs. What I saw was deep indigo, smoldering with desire so intense that I shuddered in anticipation of your touch. I felt heat from your center on my stomach, and your mouth quirked up at the corners with just a trace of a smile. You touched the tip of your tongue to my lips and traced their outline slowly before gently entering to begin the enticing slow dance with mine. Soon my head was spinning and my breathing ragged. I shifted my pelvis, trying to bring you into tighter contact with my torso. You began a slow thrusting motion that left me desperate to feel your heated sex gripping my fingers. With the pad of one finger I traced your contours with light caresses, carefully avoiding the sensitive tip of your clitoris as you moaned softly in my ear. Your hand stole down my abdomen, sliding into my sensitive folds.

Your tongue flicked my stiffened nipple to the same rhythm as your finger at my center. I drove my hands into your thick hair and pulled you more firmly against my breast, forcing it into your mouth. Soon you turned your attention to the other breast, sliding your tongue across the valley between them as you moved, to perform the same ritual, alternately sucking, nipping, devouring while your finger continued to exquisitely torment the base of my clit. My blood roared in my head with the overload of glorious sensation that radiated through every nerve ending of my body. This was life itself. Life we might have lost.

I felt the delicious tingle of my building climax ripple from my stomach toward my center, the pressure intensified with each practiced stroke from you. Coherent thought became impossible as the buzzing in my brain blocked out any other sensations save your incredible touch. Both of us moaned with pleasure. Knowing your body, your need, I slid two fingers smoothly inside and your clit jumped and throbbed against my thumb. You shifted again, forcing my fingers deeper inside. You took my nipple in your mouth, and I felt the vibration of your satisfied chuckle against my breast as your superb torment drew a new gasp from my throat.

I leaned my head back and could hear us driving each other to orgasm through the water. Our arm movements made soft whooshing sounds. The combination of sensations and sounds sent my body soaring toward climax and your pulsing muscles gripped and pulled me more firmly inside. Deeper. Harder. Yes. You dropped your head to my shoulder as I cradled you in my lap. The physical release gave way to a tenderness that threatened to undo me altogether, and I fought tears that burned my eyes. My hand was still inside you, feeling your tremors slowly fade. You wrapped your arms tightly around me and I surrendered completely into your certain embrace. You painted feather-light kisses along my neck and collarbone until I finally stilled. I raised my head to look into your amazing eyes, now a soft satisfied blue that gently gazed at me, and I was overcome once again by the depth of our love.

You smiled sweetly and placed a delicate kiss on my lips.

Then you whispered, "Welcome home."

FUZZPLOITATION

Kris Adams

It's a scorcher in the mad city. Hustlers plod through sticky asphalt to make that paper. Kids break into fire hydrants for relief, 5-0 be damned. Hookers advertise their expertise on Popsicles, their ever-watchful pimps keeping cool in the corner stores. Through the noise and haze comes a fine-ass sister, sauntering into Boss Charlie's bar like she owns the whole street. Her armor: platform boots, paisley handkerchief top, pink hot pants and a full-length chinchilla coat. Ninety-eight degrees in the shade, and she doesn't even break a sweat.

Charlie's thugs in the back room are too busy counting bags of drugs to notice the six-foot-tall (with boots and 'fro) sister watching them from the doorway. Once they see her, they spring into action, wanting to know what this foxy Black bitch is doing in the boss's hideout.

One of the goons has the audacity to place his meaty white paw on her. "Foxy broad like you will make a ton of dough for the boss." He snickers. "Maybe I'll just sample the merchandise first. You like vanilla, baby?"

"First," she says calmly, smiling so they don't notice the two shiny objects she's slipping from her purse, "you assholes are all under arrest." Before they can reach for their illegal weapons, she flashes her badge and lodges her pistol against the meat paw's noggin. "And second...I ain't your baby!" The goons make a play, like they always do. The first three get it in the chest. The fourth, in the back. She's about to take out the fifth when number six clocks her, making her drop her piece. Lip swelling, she lets the chinchilla slide to the floor before crouching into a low stance and lets loose a barrage of fast punches and strikes to disarm them. The roundhouse kicks that send them flying into the walls, those are for messing up the kisser. She's just about to finish them off when a bloated, middle-aged white man in a powder blue leisure suit comes out of a hidden door.

"Congratulations, Eboni Slicke. You've solved my over-employment problem." He laughs, clapping his sweaty hands. Before Eboni can reach for her second gun, someone grabs her from behind. She squirms, but whoever's got her is strong... skilled...and smells damn good.

"You won't get away with this, Boss Charlie!" Eboni hisses.

"But I already have." He laughs again as Eboni struggles to break free. "Let me introduce you. Detective Eboni Slicke, say hello to my new right-hand man—Fiona."

Eboni finally wriggles free and spins around to find herself looking down the barrels of both her guns. The woman holding them offers a lopsided grin, to which Eboni snaps, "Who the fuck are you?"

"I'm your worst nightmare, sweetheart," drawls Fiona, the new soldier, now number two on the detective's shit list. Eboni sizes her up: tall, hazel eyes, long brown hair, luscious mouth, tight body, white. *Shit.*

"Detective Slicke has been after me for years," Boss Charlie says. "Thinks a man ain't entitled to make a living anymore."

"Not when your living is selling drugs, turning out our women and sending our men to early graves!" Eboni points an angry finger at The Man, the scourge of her beloved city. "I'm gonna take you down if it's the last thing I do."

Charlie's evil grin widens. "Couldn't have said it better myself." Tapping Fiona on the ass, Charlie kicks aside the remains of one of his goons on his way out the door. "Take care of Miss Slicke for me, darling."

Fiona watches him go, then aims right at Eboni's mountainous hair.

"Tell me, Miss Slicke," Fiona teases, "how do you get your afro so big?"

"Why don't you put those guns down and I'll show you?" Eboni hisses, ready to open up another can of kung-fu whoop-ass.

"I've heard about you. Badass sister thinks she can take on all the crime in the city by herself." Fiona lowers the guns just a little, the smirk dropping momentarily from her face. "You're gonna get yourself killed, Slicke."

"You threatening me, white girl?"

Fiona's cocky grin returns. "You gonna do something about it?"

Eboni takes a step forward, fists at the ready.

Fiona licks her lips in anticipation and then laughs at the sound of approaching police sirens. "Looks like you don't get your man this time."

Fiona backs away, guns still trained expertly at Eboni's body. "Or should I say, you don't get your *woman?*"

As Eboni watches Fiona's nicely round ass disappear into the shadows, she contemplates how she'll explain to her captain yet another pile of dead bodies left in her wake.

* * *

Two hours of forced desk duty is all Eboni can take. She needs to be out working her cases. She needs to be out busting heads. She needs some peace and quiet.

"When are you gonna give a brother a chance, Slicke?"

"Girl, your ass is too fine to be getting shot at!"

"Just give me five minutes alone in a cell with that!"

"You couldn't even handle this," she tells the uniforms, the plainclothes, the perps being led to the lockup. Like she's supposed to go off with the first jive turkey that smiles at her. Sitting back with her platforms on her desk, she picks at her 'fro and wonders how she's supposed to nail Boss Charlie now. The paperwork doesn't tell her anything new. The only thing new in this case is that heifer that got the drop on her.

"Okay, Miss Thing," Eboni growls to herself, "I'm coming for *you* next."

Behind the wheel of her black Buick Electra 225, Eboni waits down the street from Boss Charlie's favorite hangout. Eventually the gangster and his old lady emerge, pausing to share an awkward kiss before leaving in separate cars. Cursing, Eboni tails Fiona to a modest house in a modest neighborhood. She settles in for what she expects will be a boring stakeout.

After twenty minutes of surveillance, Eboni lowers her binoculars just long enough to switch out the 8-track in the dash. When she looks back, Fiona is gone.

"Where the hell did she go?" Eboni jumps at a heavy tap on the passenger window.

"You wanna turn down the Bobby Womack?" Fiona asks sarcastically, flipping her long hair and smirking through the window at Eboni's astonished face. "People in this neighborhood are trying to sleep." Her eyes sparkle under the bright streetlamps, Eboni notices, reluctantly. "So...you gonna open the door?"

"How did you...damn." It's unlike Eboni Slicke to be at a loss for words. She'd love nothing more than to lecture this Barbie doll on everything from African decolonization to the war in Vietnam. Instead, she unlocks the door, shaking her head. "There's a warrant out for you, girlie."

"Sure there is." Fiona sinks into the passenger seat, runs her hands over the interior. "Deuce and a quarter. Nice."

Eboni raises an eyebrow. "What, you used to date a brother?"

Fiona sits back, making herself comfortable. "I used to date a lot of people."

"And now you date Boss Charlie. Were you born with a silver spoon in your mouth, then to make Daddy mad you ran off with a bunch of convicts or joined the Moonies or became a communist or something?"

"Smart *and* funny! I like that."

Eboni bristles. "What do you want?"

"Listen to me, Slicke." The smile falls away and Fiona leans closer, her voice lowering when she murmurs, "If you know what's good for you, you'll stay out of Boss Charlie's hair...or you'll be sorry."

"That's the second time you've threatened me. I could take you in for that alone."

Fiona's cocky grin returns. "I'd like to see you try—'specially since you're supposed to be on desk duty. What would your captain think?"

"How did—damn it." Eboni shakes her head, wondering which of the idiots down at the station let that precious information loose out on the street. "Whatever. I'm done playing for tonight. Now get the fuck out."

"Yes ma'am." Fiona gives a little salute before stepping out of the car. "Hope to...play with you again soon, Detective Slicke."

"Bitch." Eboni guns the 3.5L, but she stays to watch Fiona sashay back into the house before she pulls away.

A week of tailing Boss Charlie's new moll around the city gets Eboni nowhere. Desperate for a lead, she heads back to Fiona's house. The captain will have Eboni's badge if she's caught breaking and entering, but she's too close to stop now.

She's elbow-deep in Fiona's underwear drawer when she hears keys in the front door. She tiptoes into the bedroom closet, hiding behind long hippy dresses and bell bottoms as voices come from the entryway.

"C'mon, Fiona. How long you gonna hold out on me?" It's Boss Charlie, sounding well annoyed. "I promote you out of the ranks, make you my second, and for what? So you can give me blue balls?"

Fiona lets go an exaggerated sigh. "Not tonight, Charlie."

Good, Eboni thinks, before she catches herself, wondering, *What do I care who she fucks?*

"I need to make some calls about the new shipment tomorrow. Good night, Charlie." The door slams shut, Fiona makes a beeline for the bathroom and Eboni sees her chance to split—but she doesn't budge. She's never been afraid of anyone, least of all a smartass hoodlum white girl. So why she's cowering in the closet, she doesn't know. The questions racing in her head come to a screeching halt when Fiona trudges into the bedroom completely naked.

Eboni freezes, moving only her eyes as she peers through the closet door slats. She watches Fiona brush her long hair, rub night cream on her face, down her neck, between her breasts.

Eboni bites her lip, reminding herself why she's here, who Fiona is...*what* she is. That it's all in a day's work, sneaking into this outlaw's house, fingering her unmentionables and watching her slowly, slowly run long fingers across naked skin while standing in front of a full-length mirror. Eboni wants to punch herself; she squints to get a better look instead.

Fiona must be about five-ten, Eboni decides, remembering those slim, strong arms holding her tightly the first time they met. So she's half an inch taller, but Eboni has a bigger rack. The nipples are roughly the same size as Eboni's, though lighter in color. They harden as Fiona massages her breasts, her head thrown back, her eyes closed. Eboni leans closer for a better look, in case she misses something important...for the case. She might have to add to her report that Fiona likes to smooth lotion all over her naked body at bedtime. The D.A. might have to know that the hair between Fiona's legs is thicker and curlier than that on her head. Eboni might need to testify on the stand how sinuously Fiona slides onto her bed with her hands between her legs.

It's a bit surreal, Eboni realizes, to be a police detective hiding in the closet of a suspect that she's investigating, watching that suspect touch herself. Even more surreal, Eboni can't help wishing she could see more. From her position she can only view Fiona in profile: one fluttering eyelid, a tightly squeezed breast, one long, tanned thigh.

"Fuck."

Eboni winces before she realizes it wasn't her voice, though it could have been, as hot as she's getting just watching Fiona pull at her nipples and slide shaking hands over her belly. View obscured, Eboni can only imagine the rest; how swollen and moist Fiona's vulva is...if her clitoris is well-hooded or exposed and slick...how many fingers she's using to fill her vagina.

"Yes," Fiona continues, "fuck me."

Eboni wants to cross her legs. No room for that. Only room in her head, imagining what Fiona would look like in front of her, spread apart and hard and wet, what she would smell like... what she would taste like.

The detective is so busy imagining that she nearly misses Fiona climaxing with a squealed, "Oh...Eboni!"

Soon after, the bedside light goes off, and Fiona's sighs turn to the soft purrs of sleep. It takes some time, but Eboni eventually crawls out of the closet, out of the bedroom and out of the house.

After a reckless drive home, Eboni stumbles to her bedroom, leaving a trail of clothes on the way, hand sliding into her panties as soon as she hits the bed. She's mortified to find herself still wet, even more so to find that she's picturing Fiona's soft breasts and tight ass as she strokes herself. On her knees, thighs spread, aching nipples crushed to the sheets, Eboni fucks herself and can almost picture that luscious bitch kneeling underneath her, mouth open and buried between her legs.

When she allows herself to replay Fiona's last words, Eboni comes like a freight train.

For the first time since getting promoted to detective, Eboni Slicke is nose-deep in paperwork and not complaining about it. Something's going down tonight, and she will be damned if she's not there when it does. If going through every last report on this case will give her a clue, so be it. And if fixating on the job keeps her mind off last night's activities, even better.

She's so engrossed in her work that she barely takes notice of an unfamiliar messenger delivering a plainly wrapped package. Eboni rips it open absentmindedly, only noticing when she's down to the box and tissue paper that whatever is inside is moving.

It's not a bomb. She's had enough experience with nut cases in the city to know that. Whatever it is can't be good, and if she wasn't so distracted lately she'd never have opened an unmarked package by herself. Too late for gloves, her prints are all over it now. Carefully, she pushes aside the mass of tissue paper and peers inside.

"Fuck me." Eboni stares at the box for a minute until the blood runs back into her face and she can breathe. When she's collected herself, she removes the attached note card and reads:

Miss Slicke,

I hope this note finds you well, and that you'll heed my warning about the Boss. Give up and you'll have nothing to worry your pretty little head about.

Yours,
F

P.S. After your little Peeping Tom stint last night, I thought you could use this.

Eboni reads the note a third time before crumpling it and shoving the box, tissues and still-humming vibrator into her bottom desk drawer.

"That's it," the detective growls to herself, "I'm taking these suckas out tonight."

Eboni knows someone's broken into her place as soon as she steps out of the shower. She would be impressed if she wasn't so pissed off. Ignoring her robe, she walks right into her bedroom and heads for her dresser. As expected, the sight of her beautiful naked blackness elicits a complimentary whistle.

"You must have a death wish coming here," Eboni murmurs, her back to the intruder but her defenses high. Slowly she opens her underwear drawer and feels around for the—

"You looking for this?" The sound of her .38 cocking sends Eboni spinning around, and for the second time in a week she's face-to-face with Fiona holding her own gun on her. Fiona smiles, but at least has the decency to blush as her eyes fall over Eboni's body.

"It's only fair," Fiona explains, though she has to clear her throat first. "Since you broke into my place last night. That wasn't very nice, Detective. Wasn't very legal, either."

"What do you know about legal?"

"What do you know about *me*, Slicke?"

"You're a criminal. That's all I need to know."

"You know more than that. You know where I live...where I hang out...and you know what I sound like when I come...don't you?"

"I don't know what you're talking about," Eboni mumbles, cocky as ever, even though her pulse quickens and her stomach flutters.

"Did you like that little show of mine last night?" Fiona comes closer, gun still trained on her target. "I bet you did. I bet you thought it was real, didn't you?"

Eboni lets her eyes go soft, slouches a little. "So, you didn't really..."

Something changes in Fiona's demeanor. She points the gun at the floor, comes a few steps closer. "Well, maybe I did and maybe I didn't. Maybe I liked you watching me." A little closer, and Eboni puts on her best come-hither smile.

"Maybe I liked watching," purrs the detective.

Fiona licks her lips and takes another step, giving Eboni the chance to kick the gun deftly out of her hand. "Okay, white girl. Let's dance."

Five minutes later, the crib is wrecked and both ladies are bruised and exhausted. Eboni refuses to give in, but she's running out of steam, so goes for the easy target—Fiona's long hair.

"Ow! No fair!"

"Shut up," Eboni roars as she wrestles Fiona by her hair and pins her to the ground. "It's over. Tell me why you're here."

Fiona laughs as she catches her breath, continuing to struggle, but clearly exhausted. "I'm here to tell you to get out of town. Right now."

"Why?"

"Because Boss Charlie sent me here to get rid of you."

Eboni is too pleased to finally have something to take to the D.A. to even bother feeling frightened. "What's stopping you?"

"You on top of me."

Eboni looks down at her nakedness and blushes, hoping to god that Fiona hasn't noticed that she has been horny as hell since they started fighting. By the way Fiona's eyes slide down to between her legs, yeah, she knows.

"Aw, hell." Eboni sits back, relieving the pressure on Fiona's wrists, but she doesn't let go, not even when Fiona arches upward, pressing her face between Eboni's breasts, her thigh between Eboni's legs.

"Tell me something, Detective." Fiona smiles shyly as she nudges Eboni's left breast with her nose, rubbing her swollen lips around the nipple until Eboni gasps her approval. "Do you like vanilla?"

"I'm starting to." Eboni tries to hold back a moan when she feels a hot open mouth on her nipples and possessive hands on her ass. But when Fiona brushes nervous hands over Eboni's face, touches her full lips and whispers "what a fine-ass sistah," Eboni gives in. She kisses Fiona hard, impatiently, riled up by the fighting and the flirting. Thankfully Fiona doesn't say *I told you so*. She's too busy sucking Eboni's tongue into her mouth to talk, too busy squeezing Eboni's full breasts to fight, too busy grinding herself against Eboni's crotch to run away.

Standing quickly to pull her dress over her head, Fiona leans in, giving Eboni her belly to kiss, her ass to knead, her body to possess. Eboni starts with one breast, cupping it possessively as she licks circles over the sensitive nipple. When she adds a bit of teeth, Fiona squeals and yanks gracelessly on her panties. Eboni pulls them down slowly so she can revel at the damp spot on the crotch. She pulls Fiona to her, rubbing her nose and lips over the curly pubic hair, almost as curly as hers. Just a bit closer, and she's kissing Fiona's lips, licking at the swollen labia until Fiona growls and pulls away, breathing hard.

"Bedroom," Fiona purrs, pulling Eboni quickly through the broken lamps and overturned furniture. She sinks to the bed, scooting back so Eboni can kneel before her and watch as she spreads wide. Her mouth open and wet, she looks like she might burst into tears if Eboni doesn't taste her soon. Eboni touches, teases, coaxes Fiona's vulva open while she kisses her inner thighs.

"Eboni…god…I wasn't faking last night. I swear."

Eboni giggles with the realization that she doesn't care one way or the other. Still, it's nice to hear. She rewards Fiona with long, slow tongue strokes up and down the cleft of Venus before spearing her, sliding her tongue deep into Fiona's warm vagina. She digs in for more, sucking and licking the skin over Fiona's clitoris until Fiona squeals and grabs at Eboni's head.

"Watch the 'fro."

"Sorry." Fiona settles for grabbing Eboni's shoulders, her

face, anything to get more lips, more tongue, more everything. When she looks down and sees Eboni stroking herself, she hisses, "Hurry...so I can do you."

Eboni curses and wets her forefinger, then presses it against Fiona's vagina, watching intently as she enters her, feeling the heat inside. With Fiona's legs lifted off the bed, Eboni can reach inside with three fingers, fucking her deep and slow, smiling at how sticky her hand is getting. Once she starts sucking steady and fast on Fiona's clit, it's all over. She keeps it up, fingers fast and tongue faster, until Fiona screams her arrival.

"Not bad for a white—"

"I'll show you not bad," Fiona hisses. She pushes Eboni on her back quickly, but takes her time touching her.

Eboni squirms as white hands learn her curves, fondle her nipples and massage her calves.

"Spread your legs. I want to see the motherland."

Any other time Eboni would burst out laughing, but she's too turned on now. Right now everything coming out of Fiona's mouth sounds like heaven. So she sits up and leans on one elbow as she rubs long, trigger-ready fingers over her mons.

"Lemme see," Fiona whispers.

Eboni gladly spreads her labia with her fingers, exposing herself to Fiona's inquisitive eyes.

"Yeah," Fiona whispers, licking her lips at the blackness, the pinkness, the wetness. "You like vanilla, all right."

"Fuck, yes." Eboni reaches out, but Fiona is on her right away, licking all over Eboni's genitals, sucking on the hood of her clitoris, teasing the vagina until it coats the tip of her tongue.

"Don't stop, Fiona, don't stop."

"Wow. You've never said my name before."

Their eyes meet, and suddenly Eboni feels scared, in a way she hasn't since the last time she fell for someone.

"I like that." Fiona stops what she's doing to crawl up into a searing kiss. Eboni tastes herself in Fiona's mouth, thinks that's where her flavor belongs. She holds Fiona to her. They're both shaking. "Can't believe I'm in bed with Boss Charlie's girl," Eboni admits under her breath.

"Fuck Charlie." Fiona looks her adversary-cum-lover straight in the eye. "Fuck him," she growls as she spreads Eboni's thighs wider and slides between, pressing her pussy, still hot and wet, against Eboni's pubic bone. She tilts and arches slowly, so Eboni can feel her inch by inch, until their clits touch and both women gasp.

"Oh...fuck me," Eboni demands breathlessly in her *I-will-bust-a-cap-in-your-ass* voice.

"With pleasure." Fiona kisses her way back down Eboni's quivering body, stopping momentarily to suck Eboni's nipples while her fingers continue their descent. "You feel so good," she purrs after slipping two fingers inside.

Eboni urges her on with arched back and wanton moans. Then long white fingers slip out of her to make way for one flattened pink tongue.

"Mmm...chocolate." Fiona's words become garbled as she sinks farther in, lapping at Eboni's hard clit and fucking her with as much of her hand as Eboni can take until she starts to shake. "Yeah. C'mon," Fiona grunts, working faster, her hands and tongue nearly in sync with Eboni's gyrations. "Yes. Wanted this when I first saw you, baby."

"Me, too." The admission is too much. Eboni closes her eyes, squeezes Fiona with her legs, her arms, her pussy, and lets go.

Eboni could kick herself for falling asleep. If she hadn't, they would have probably gone another round. And, she wouldn't have ended up handcuffed to her bedpost.

"I knew it," she barks as she tugs at her own handcuffs—the only things keeping her from wringing Fiona's neck. "This was all just a setup."

Fiona smiles sweetly as she peruses the bedroom for the rest of her clothes. "I told you, Eboni. Boss Charlie's out to get you. This way, you stay safe." She leans down to kiss the detective, who turns away petulantly. "You won't have to worry about him after tonight."

"What do you mean? Is it that shipment you were talking about last night? Tell me!"

Fiona shrugs and heads for the door.

"Where are my car keys?" Eboni shouts. "I'll be out of these cuffs in no time and then I'll be after you."

"Well, I better take these with me, then." Stuffing Eboni's keys into her pocket, Fiona takes a last look at the detective she keeps besting. "I'm really sorry about this, sweetheart. I know you want this. But I want it, too." She pushes her hair behind her ear and whispers, "I want a lot of things."

Eboni waits until Fiona's been gone sixty seconds and then she jumps off the bed, disengages the headboard, drags it across the room to the phone, knocks the receiver to the floor and dials with her big toe.

"Captain," she yells down at the phone, "send a black-and-white over to my place—and activate that bug that I keep on my keychain!"

Within the hour, a horde of uniformed police are swooping in to surround the warehouse to which Fiona unknowingly led them. Eboni Slicke stands by proudly as Boss Charlie's henchmen scatter, only to be swiftly taken into custody. She's almost disappointed that she doesn't have to shoot anyone.

"You won't get away with this," Boss Charlie spits as an

officer attempts to cuff him. He turns an accusatory eye at Fiona, who stands obediently with hands raised. "You flipped on me, didn't you?"

Fiona rolls her eyes, though she looks a little pissed. "I do that a lot."

"You got that right," says Eboni under her breath, eyes fixed on Fiona.

Boss Charlie follows the intense gaze between the two women, and then he starts to laugh. "Oh, *now* I get it. You're not frigid—you're a rug muncher! I shoulda known."

"I didn't screw you because you disgust me," Fiona snarls. "I wouldn't touch you with a ten-foot pole."

Eboni giggles despite herself. "Three-inch pole, from what I hear."

Before Fiona can respond, "Got that right," Boss Charlie head-butts the cop behind him, shakes out of the unlocked cuffs, grabs the uniform's gun and points it directly at Eboni's head.

It happens so fast, the other cops don't have time to react before Boss Charlie pulls the trigger. Eboni dives like a champion, just in case The Man gets lucky and she's done for. When she recovers, Boss Charlie is dead on the floor and Fiona is standing over him holding the only smoking gun in the room. The other officers shout orders, weapons aimed right at Fiona's vitals, until she very calmly drops the gun and pulls out a piece of leather from her blouse.

"It's all right," Fiona shouts as she holds up a badge. "I'm an undercover cop."

"I guess we should talk."

Eboni doesn't look up from her station desk, just keeps typing up her notes. "Everything you need to know will be in my report," she grumbles.

"Everything?" Fiona slides carefully onto Eboni's desk, pulling her dress up enough to show just a peek of the panties Eboni ripped off her hours earlier. "Don't forget to add the part where you made me come in under three minutes."

Eboni huffs and stops typing. "Two."

Fiona scoots closer, her leg brushing against Eboni's arm. "You can trust me, you know."

"Can't do that, Fiona. I don't know anything real about you."

"I'm a cop. I'm overworked and underpaid and I've almost died more times than I can count." Fiona touches Eboni's hand, and both women blush at the electricity between them. "And I love my job. I get to serve the public, and I get to bring down assholes like Boss Charlie. And...I got to meet you."

"Damn. No wonder you're so good undercover."

"It's true. You're a great cop." Fiona licks her lips and murmurs, "You're great at a lot of things."

Eboni can't help smiling. Fiona's sitting too close. "So, what do you want?"

"I want to talk shop with you," Fiona replies softly yet decisively. "I want to go to target practice with you." She slides her knee underneath Eboni's forearm, hissing when the detective takes the hint and brushes tentative fingers on her inner thigh. "I want to taste you again, right now," she whispers. "And tomorrow and the next day, too."

Barely able to breathe, Eboni closes her eyes and tries to picture herself cruising in the 'hood, funk music booming on her stereo, dashiki on her back, with a gorgeous white chick by her side. Doesn't seem possible. And then she remembers how good it felt to fall asleep in Fiona's arms. She shuts off her typewriter.

"Well, I'm beat, and my pad is a mess."

Fiona stands and offers a hopeful smile. "I have coffee and

doughnuts at my place."

"Good." Eboni slips her fingers into Fiona's soft hand, Neapolitan minus the strawberry. "Let's go."

STUDY GROUP

Radclyffe

Could anything be worse than an empty dorm on the holidays? The echo of my solitary footsteps had me turning every few yards to see who might be coming down the hall after me—and the shower was seriously creepy. After the first night of Thanksgiving break, I'd taken to leaving the bathroom door *and* the shower door open, and washing as if water was being rationed— triple time, speed rinse.

Most of the time, I pretty much liked dorm living—okay, maybe after three months, the thrill of living away from home was starting to get a little old. I mean, it was fun, even if the university did have a freshman curfew. But the curfew was one o'clock, and at home I'd had to be in most nights by eleven, except when my father was feeling generous and said twelve thirty. Of course, he'd stopped waiting up for me to come in when I was seventeen, so that last summer before I left for school was a lot better. I wasn't really dating very much anyway, so twelve thirty was usually plenty late enough for me. I'd drive most of the time because my three best girl-friends liked to party, and drinking didn't seem to agree with me. I didn't like feeling fuzzy and out of control and I definitely didn't like puking, so being the party-pooper designated driver was no hardship.

I wasn't really into picking up guys like they were either. I'd tried that about as many times as I'd tried drinking and felt just about as disappointed afterward. Some of the guys were decent kissers and the few times I'd gone further than that had been okay. For some reason, guys seemed to think that a clit was just a little dick and tended to handle it just the same too—rough, too fast and sort of goal oriented—like getting off was all there was to care about. Cocks were okay—not real subtle in terms of the mechanics, but then that was fine with me. A few strokes, a couple of tugs and they were good to go. They were happy, I was kind of glad to be done with it and that was that. So after the first few times, I wasn't really interested in a repeat.

Once I got to school, I didn't have time to worry about partying or dating guys. I was pre-med, so that pretty much said it all. According to my mom, who's a surgeon, it wasn't quite as hard to get into medical schools as it used to be, but I still wanted to have my pick of schools and I planned on having really good grades. I studied a lot and didn't hang with too many of my dorm mates.

The dorms were divided up into four suites at the corner of every floor, each with two bedrooms and a common study area. Every floor had its own central lounge shared by all the residents in the suites on that floor. My roommate, Shar, was into art, and even though we didn't have much in common, we'd gotten tight really fast. Sometimes I'd catch her looking at me with a thoughtful expression, like she was waiting for me to figure something out, but when I'd say *What?* she'd just shake her head with a little smile that made me feel clueless and a little tingly all at once.

Shar and I were the only students on our floor who hadn't gone home for Thanksgiving break. My parents had a chance to go away on some cruise, and since my mom didn't usually have a lot of time off, I told them they should go. I could've flown to California and spent the holiday with my grandparents, but it seemed like a long way to go for a few days, and I could use the time to study. I wasn't exactly behind, but it was always good to be ahead.

I don't know why Shar stayed at school, but I figured it had something to do with her girlfriend Andi, who lived halfway across the country. Andi's parents were freaked about her being queer, so I guess she didn't want to go home alone—and Shar wasn't welcome. The two of them hadn't been out of Shar's room much since Wednesday afternoon after everyone else left. If I'd had a steady...somebody...I'd probably want to be doing it 24/7 too. Last night had been a little tricky, though. Shar was loud when she came, and she was coming almost all night. At one point I thought about sleeping on the couch in the lounge, but then I would've been embarrassed because they'd know I could hear them. And besides that, I kinda liked hearing them. Okay, I liked hearing them a lot.

Shar talked when she got excited, so it's not like I had to try hard to hear what was happening. The closer she got to coming, the more she directed Andi to do her just so.

That's it, baby, oh yeah put your mouth right there. Suck my clit. Lick me now, baby. You'll make me come, oh fuck oh god I'm going to come in your mouth.

And so on. Over and over. She just kept on and on about how good it felt, how close she was getting, and Andi would be groaning and chanting *Come, baby, come. Oh yeah, all over me, come, baby.*

After an hour of that I was so freaking turned on I had to come myself. I'd seen girls kissing before, and I'm pretty sure I saw Nancy Tucker get off with her girlfriend at a party, but they weren't making much noise and I felt a little perverted watching them. But it's not like I could do anything about hearing Shar and Andi. I don't think Shar would really care if I got off listening to her come. So I did. A couple of times. Okay, four times. In fact, thinking about it was getting me turned on again, and advanced calculus really wasn't much of a problem for me. It's not like I really had to do that right now.

I pushed back my chair and shoved my hand in my sweats. Oh yeah. Wet and hard. This wouldn't take long. I closed my eyes and conjured up the sound of Shar screaming *I have to come, I have to come, oh my god I'm coming.* I stroked the sides of my clit and felt the buzz in my belly. Oh yeah.

A knock shook the door. Shar's voice. "Hey? You want to watch a movie with us?"

A movie. I tried to think through the pre-orgasmic haze. That would probably be sociable and everything, but geez, I was so horny and so ready to come.

"We got pizza," Andi called.

Fuck.

"Okay." I opened the door. "Yeah, sure. Thanks."

Shar grinned. She was pretty. Black hair, dark eyebrows, bright blue eyes, pouty mouth. Hot piercings—one in the corner of her left eyebrow and a whole row in one ear. I wondered if there were more, but I'd never seen her completely naked. I'd see her bare ass just out of the shower a few times, and it was a nice ass. Round and tight and I thought about how it might feel to hold her ass while she was moaning and...

Well, I couldn't go down that road while I was looking right at her. My face must've shown something because she grinned, a really sexy grin that made my clit jump. Andi was leaning in the doorway with a sixteen-inch pizza box in her hand. She was tall and thin. Short red hair, a few freckles, green eyes. She had a basketball scholarship. From a distance, she kinda looked like a guy, but up close, she didn't. She had small breasts and slender hips, but her face was really striking, with elegant features like the profiles on those old-style cameos. I shot her an *Is company okay with you?* look and she grinned too. Andi was like that— easy to be around, with a way of looking at you that made you feel like she was really paying attention. Like you mattered.

"Well, if there's enough," I muttered, and I wasn't even sure if I was talking about the pizza.

"Plenty." Andi threw an arm around my shoulder. "Like mushroom and buffalo chicken pizza?"

"Yeah, I do."

"Come on. We set up the DVD in the lounge. It's just us, so we can watch it on the big screen."

"Cool," I said, following them out, walking just a little gingerly on account of my clit being so damn hard. Andi gave my shoulder a friendly squeeze and we all settled down on a big leather sofa facing the wall-screen TV.

The two of them curled up in the corner of the sofa and put the pizza box on a low coffee table in front of it. I sat on the other end and we all helped ourselves while Andi fiddled with the remote to start the movie. I took a bite of my pizza and glanced at the screen. I stopped chewing. Two women, no, three women were all tangled up together on a big bed, naked. I swallowed without chewing the rest of the bite. "Um…what's the movie?"

"Girl porn," Andi said, sliding her arm around Shar's waist and propping her legs up on the corner of the coffee table. Shar slid her hand under Andi's shirt onto her stomach.

"I love this stuff," Shar said. "It's hokey, but sometimes the girls are really cute and I love watching them go down on each other."

Oh fuck. This was going to be a problem. I wasn't just a little bit horny now, I really *really* needed to get off. And the two of them were getting awfully cozy.

"Have you ever seen this kinda stuff before?" Shar asked, delicately nibbling her way along the edges of a slice of pizza. She had this way of teasing the gooey cheese off with the tip of her tongue, drawing it out in long strands that clung to the edges of her lips and then pursing her lips and sucking it in. Every bite was a process. I imagined her tongue sliding between the lips of my pussy, drawing shiny strands of come from deep inside me and swallowing it down. My clit twitched, jumping up and down, anticipating the way her lips would close around me, sucking delicately. My stomach went hard as a board.

"No, but it looks like fun." I sounded a little bit like a robot, like one of those electronic telemarketers that leaves canned messages on your answering machine. I felt a little bit like a dork too, but no way was I leaving. Not when Shar's hand was climbing up to Andi's breasts under her T-shirt. I put the slice of pizza down on a paper napkin. I couldn't even pretend to eat, not with what was going down on the screen and right next to me.

Andi had obviously started the thing in the middle or knew where the good parts were. The three girls were propped up side by side, the two on the outside masturbating the one in the middle. They took turns kissing her while they jerked her off together, both of them working their clits with their free hands at the same time. I really wanted to be the one in the middle. I wanted Shar on one side of me and Andi on the other, their fingers stroking over my pussy, teasing my clit, while they kissed me and sucked my nipples. Alternating between watching the screen and watching Shar and Andi, who were making out like crazy now, had me so keyed up I was ready to come in my sweats. Shar was making those little high-pitched whines she makes when she gets really excited and Andi was muttering *You're so hot, babe, you're so hot you're gonna come all over me.*

I thought maybe I should leave, but when I edged toward the end of the couch, Shar grabbed my arm.

"Don't you like the movie?"

"I like the movie," I said, panting a little bit. "I just figured you might want to be alone."

"We invited you, remember? Come on over here and get more comfortable."

Andi had Shar's shirt pushed up so her breasts were exposed. Shar had truly beautiful breasts. Small, tight pink nipples perfectly placed in the center of firm, medium-sized breasts— like cherries on top of a gorgeous sundae. I wanted to lick her. I'd never really gotten into oral sex before, but I wanted those nipples in my mouth. Shar worked her hand inside Andi's sweats and I watched her stroke Andi's pussy through the thin fabric. I wanted her fingers on my clit.

Maybe this was why I hadn't minded not dating the last six months. I wondered why it had taken me so long to figure it out. Blame it on pre-med tunnel vision, I guess. I pushed across the couch toward them like my ass was on fire.

"What should I do?" I said.

Shar glanced at Andi, who nodded. "Anything you want."

I kissed Shar, and she tasted like cheese and tomato sauce and her tongue was spicy when it slid into my mouth. I was lost somewhere in Shar's soft heat when Andi untied my sweats, stroked the bare strip of skin between my T-shirt and my sweats, and worked her way down. My clit got tight and I moaned into Shar's mouth. Shar writhed against me and Andi rolled my clit between her fingers. Another minute, she'd make me come.

"Wait," I gasped, turning my head to kiss Andi. She kissed differently than Shar, no teasing, just taking, deep and hard. "I'll come."

"No harm, no foul," Andi murmured and slid inside me. My hips surged on their own, lifting against Andi's hand. I wanted to come on her so bad.

Shar shifted to my other side and I was in the middle. She sucked my nipple and Andi's tongue was in my mouth and her fingers were between my legs and everything was happening so fast. I arched off the couch, my head and my ass the only parts touching.

"Oh my god, you're gonna make me explode."

Shar laughed, her mouth against my breast.

Andi ran her tongue along the side of my ear. "You're so wet, and your clit is really pumped. You're gonna come so hard."

I whimpered. No one had ever touched me the way Andi touched me now, like her fingers knew exactly the spots that got me off. I was really close and then she moved away from my clit and I whimpered again.

Shar murmured, "Don't worry, she'll make you come. She's amazing."

"You too, baby," Andi said to Shar, circling my clit with one fingertip, "you come too."

"Oh yeah." Shar moaned and straddled my leg. She'd shed her pants, I don't know when, and her pussy was hot and so wet.

I cupped Shar's breasts and plucked her cherry nipples. My clit knotted under Andi's finger and started to tingle. So so close now. I licked at Andi's lip. "I want to come so bad."

Shar rode me while she sucked on my breast and Andi kissed me and slid her fingers in and out of me and I knew I was gonna come. No way could I not come with Andi filling me up and Shar teasing my nipples and working her pussy off on my leg. My clit tightened and my stomach went hard and the buzzing deep in my pussy spread to my legs and my ass.

"Oh my god," I moaned, and Andi stroked my clit faster between her thumb and fingers and Shar sucked me and I kissed Andi and started coming. I jerked and Shar screamed she was coming and Andi groaned and thrust her pussy against my hip. I didn't know where I stopped and they started, or which orgasm belonged to whom, and it didn't matter. We were connected and the pleasure was everyone's.

I'm not sure how long I came or how many times Shar and Andi did, or who did what to who, but when I looked at the screen again the movie was over and the three of us were wrapped up together and covered in come.

"That was amazing," I said.

Shar's head was on my shoulder and I was curled with my back against Andi's chest, her arm around my waist.

"Yeah, it was," Shar crooned.

"Awesome," Andi muttered.

"We weren't sure you were into girls." Shar laughed a little. "We just sort of hoped."

"I am." I sighed. "I'm just kind of a slow learner."

"Oh, no, you're not." Andi squeezed the back of my neck in a way that made me feel safe and horny at the same time. "You're like in advanced class already."

"I wouldn't mind majoring in queer studies," I said, hoping they might like the idea. I wanted more time with them, both of them. And not just for the sex, which was so good my mind was kind of melting, but because I liked the idea of...us. "I mean, if the two of you wanted..."

"We've been talking about finding a study partner, but we

wanted someone special." Shar stroked my face and when her breasts rubbed mine, I got hard again. She kissed Andi across my body. "Right, baby?"

"Uh-huh." Andi cupped my breast and tugged on my nipple, shooting a charge straight to my clit. Then she kissed me, really softly, and I knew we were all connected, like Shar had said, someplace special. "I think we'll make an awesome threesome. Oh yeah—and a great study group."

I rolled on top of Shar and kissed her. Andi skated her hand down the center of my back and stroked my ass. I couldn't wait for the rest of the semester to start.

A BOI'S LOVE SONG

Kathleen Tudor

My hands shake as I push the cufflinks through their holes, one emerald green, one amber topaz. Her idea. Her gift to me. Her birthstone and mine. My brother shakes his head at me, but he doesn't tell me again that it's silly, sappy or too sweet. He just tweaks my bowtie into alignment and holds up my jacket.

"Mom's gonna be pissed that you get to be a groom before me," he teases.

I shrug to settle the jacket. "I'm not a groom. I'm just a different kind of bride."

He snorts and puts out his hand for a handshake. I pull him into a hug. Ten minutes. *Oh god, oh god, oh god...*

I can't remember what I was going to say to her. I grope for the vows I wrote as Tommy leads me to the chapel. My hands feel clammy and sweaty, and my head feels flushed and light. I am *not* going to faint in the middle of this church. The words swirl, out of reach, until the first lines of my heartfelt outpouring float to the surface. *Oh, right...*

"I knew from the first moment I saw you that you were way too good for me. I'm glad I never let that stop me, or I would have cheated myself out of loving the most brilliant, beautiful and incredible woman I've ever met." I'd almost decided on *busty*. I left it out, but now I'm nervous that I'll say it in front of everyone. *Oh god…* "You're everything I'm not, and you give me the strength to be strong for you. But the thing is, you're really the strongest woman I know; way stronger than I could ever imagine being.…"

I may have the muscles in our relationship, but she has the backbone of steel and the power to back up her iron will. She took me shopping for her perfect princess wedding dress, and we went from store to store until she finally found the one that made her eyes misty and her breath catch. That was when the shop girl had walked up and asked what her "brother" thought of the dress.

Anna had turned to that girl, with nary a trace of disappointment on her face—only censure—and had proudly announced that I was her future *wife,* thank you, and if she couldn't treat me with respect, then Anna would take the dress off right then, and we could go. It made my heart tremble with love to know that she meant every word and that she'd settle for a lesser dress just to shut that snide shop girl up. I was glad that she didn't have to.

My brother walks with me to the front of the church, but it feels like I stand up there alone forever, my hands clasped and trembling before me as I wish I'd given in to her urging to carry a bouquet. My brother's at my side, but it's me everyone is looking at. My family. Hers. Our friends. Everyone shifting in their seats, murmuring to their neighbor and playing with their phones. What I wouldn't give to likewise fidget! It feels like a week of statue stillness, exposed, before the vestibule door opens

and her sister steps through, looking adorable as she sways to
the front of the room in her coral gown.

I've always thought Tiff was cute, and she never missed an
opportunity to tease me—the straight girl flirting with her gay
sister's girlfriend; innocent fun—but today I can't take my eyes
off that plain wooden door, as if by looking hard enough, I can
see through it to *her*. Anna...

"It's easy to be strong when the world puts the weight on your
shoulders from your earliest years. I've never been able to hide
what I am, and as a consequence, I have always had to bear it or
break under the weight. But you look as feminine and delicate as
the world could hope for, and you could easily hide that which
is different. But you bear the same weight by choice, proudly
claiming me wherever we go. Coming out of the closet isn't something you did once and put behind you; it's something that you
do again and again, and will continue to do for the rest of your
life, showing a courage I can only envy, admire and adore."

The door finally cracks open, and there she is, beaming in
that perfect, gorgeous dress that flaunts her bare shoulders and
her tiny waist. She clings to her father's arm, and his face looks
a little misty. It takes me a moment to realize that *everything*
looks misty, and that's because I'm crying at the sight of her
as she walks slowly down the aisle, steady as can be on those
towering heels, and her eyes are fixed on my face, the way my
eyes are on hers.

I barely look at her father when he puts her hand in mine,
and as we turn to face the minister, she squeezes my hand and I
know that once again, her strength is bearing me up.

Her vows are as sweet as she is, and she promises to love
me and cherish me and keep my needs in her heart. There is
nothing there but perfect, beautiful honesty and a promise that
that sweetness will continue to be mine to sample.

It's my turn. My vows, carefully polished—my best chance to show her how much she means to me.

"You give me the courage to be your strong right arm, the bravery to stand between you and the world, wherever I can, and the heart to be proud of everything that I am. By loving me, you show me how much of me there is to love. You're the daughter my parents always wanted and the magnificent, mysterious type of woman who has always fascinated me, maybe because I always knew I would never be anything like you. You show me the strong counter-side to my every weakness, and you make me strive to be the hero that you have always seen in me. I love you, and I would be an idiot not to tell you so every single day for the rest of our lives."

As I fall silent, I hear sniffles throughout the church, but I have eyes only for Anna, whose eyes have gone shiny with tears of joy.

ABOUT THE AUTHORS

KRIS ADAMS (smadasirk.blogspot.com) writes erotica, short fiction, fan fiction and poetry. Her work has appeared in *Best Women's Erotica 2009*, *Best Lesbian Romance 2010*, *Girl Crush*, *Daily Flashes of Erotica* and *Irresistible: Erotic Romance for Couples*.

JILLIAN BOYD is a twenty-two-year-old author/blogger, based in London. She's been previously published by the likes of Constable and Robinson and Cliterati.

Called a "legendary erotica heavy-hitter" (by the über-legendary Violet Blue), **ANDREA DALE** (cyvarwydd.com) dedicates this story to mothers and daughters everywhere. Her work has appeared in about 100 anthologies from Harlequin Spice, Avon Red and Cleis Press, and is available online at Soul's Road Press.

A lover of unusual things, **CHERYL DRAGON** (cheryldragon. com) enjoys writing unique stories with sinfully hot erotic romance. Her two favorite settings are Las Vegas and New Orleans...where anything can happen!

LISA FIGUEROA is a Chicana writer from the Los Angeles area. Her fiction appears in *Lessons in Love: Erotic Interludes 3, Iridescence* and *Best Lesbian Romance 2007.*

JANE FLETCHER is author of ten speculative fiction novels. Her works have won the Golden Crown Award and the Alice B Readers Award and have been short-listed for both the Lambda and Gaylactic Spectrum Awards.

D. JACKSON LEIGH grew up barefoot and happy, swimming in farm ponds and riding rude ponies in rural Georgia. She is the author of six lesbian romances, laced with Southern humor and set against her trademark equestrian backdrop.

BRITTNEY LOUDIN is an aspiring novelist with a part-time retail gig, a handful of college credits and a passion for lesbian romantic literature.

LEE LYNCH is the author of *The Raid, Beggar of Love* and *Sweet Creek* as well as the classic titles: *The Swashbuckler, Toothpick House* and *Old Dyke Tales.* Her work has been honored with the James Duggins Mid-Career Award, among many others.

LYNETTE MAE served in the army before diving into a law enforcement career. Her life's rich experiences provide endless inspiration for stories filled with real-life action and plenty of romance.

CATHERINE MAIORISI lives in New York City and can usually be found writing in her neighborhood Starbucks. Her short story "A Matter of Justice" appeared in the anthology *Murder New York Style: Fresh Slices*.

ANNA MEADOWS is a part-time executive assistant, part-time Sapphic housewife. Her work appears in eleven Cleis Press anthologies and on the Lambda Literary website.

JADE MELISANDE (kinkandpoly.com) is a sex, kink and relationship blogger and erotica writer living in the Midwest with her two partners. She has been published in anthologies such as *Spankalicious, Show Me, Serve Him, Cheeky Spanking Stories, Voyeur Eyes Only, Orgasmic, Lesbian Lust* and *Power Play*.

JL MERROW (jlmerrow.com) is that rare beast, an English person who refuses to drink tea. Her novella *Muscling Through* was shortlisted for a 2013 EPIC ebook Award.

SARA RAUCH's writing (www.sararauch.com) has appeared in *Earth's Daughters, The Black Boot, Inkwell, The Prose-Poem Project, The Q Review, theneweryork* and in the anthology *Dear John, I Love Jane*.

JEAN ROBERTA (erotica-readers.blogspot.com) teaches English in a Canadian university and has written over ninety erotic stories, two single-author collections and a lesbian novella, *The Flight of the Black Swan*.

SHISUMA is a student and an aspiring writer whose passion is stories about women loving women.

KATHLEEN TUDOR (KathleenTudor.com) is a rockin' erotic author and super-editor, with stories in anthologies from Cleis, Circlet, Storm Moon, Mischief HarperCollins, Circlet, Xcite and more. Check her out in *Take Me, My Boyfriend's Boyfriends* and *Kiss Me at Midnight.*

ALLISON WONDERLAND (aisforallison.blogspot.com) is one L of a girl. Her lesbian literature appears in the Cleis collections *Girl Fever, Best Lesbian Romance 2013, Girls Who Score, Sudden Sex* and *Wild Girls, Wild Nights.*

ABOUT THE EDITOR

RADCLYFFE has written over forty romance and romantic intrigue novels, dozens of short stories, a paranormal romance series (writing as L.L. Raand), and has edited over a dozen anthologies including *Best Lesbian Romance 2009* through *2014*. She is an eight-time Lambda Literary Award finalist in romance, mystery and erotica—winning in both romance (*Distant Shores, Silent Thunder*) and erotica (*Erotic Interludes 2: Stolen Moments*, edited with Stacia Seaman and *In Deep Waters 2: Cruising the Strip*, written with Karin Kallmaker). A member of the Saints and Sinners Literary Hall of Fame, she is also a RWA Prism, Lories, Beanpot, Aspen Gold and Laurel Wreath winner in multiple mainstream romance categories. She is also the President of Bold Strokes Books, an independent LGBTQ publisher.

More of the Best Lesbian Romance

Best Lesbian Romance 2013
Edited by Radclyffe

Radclyffe, the *Best Lesbian Romance* series legendary editor and a bestselling romance writer herself, says it best: "Love and romance may defy simple definition, but every story in this collection speaks to the universal thread that binds lovers everywhere—possibility."
ISBN 978-1-57344-901-4 $15.95

Best Lesbian Romance 2012
Edited by Radclyffe

Best Lesbian Romance 2012 celebrates the dizzying sensation of falling in love—and the electrifying thrill of sexual passion. Romance maestra Radclyffe gathers irresistible stories of lesbians in love to awaken your desire and send your imagination soaring.
ISBN 978-1-57344-757-7 $14.95

Best Lesbian Romance 2011
Edited by Radclyffe

"*Best Lesbian Romance* series editor Radclyffe has assembled a respectable crop of 17 authors for this year's offering. The stories are diverse in tone, style and subject, each containing a satisfying, surprising twist."—*Curve*
ISBN 978-1-57344-427-9 $14.95

Best Lesbian Romance 2010
Edited by Radclyffe

Ranging from the short and ever-so-sweet to the recklessly passionate, *Best Lesbian Romance 2010* is essential reading for anyone who favors the highly imaginative, the deeply sensual, and the very loving.
ISBN 978-1-57344-376-0 $14.95

Best Lesbian Romance 2009
Edited by Radclyffe

Scale the heights of emotion and the depths of desire with this collection of the very best lesbian romance writing of the year.
ISBN 978-1-57344-333-3 $14.95

Fuel Your Fantasies

Carnal Machines
Steampunk Erotica
Edited by D. L. King

In this decadent fusing of technology and romance, outstanding contemporary erotica writers use the enthralling possibilities of the 19th-century steam age to tease and titillate.
ISBN 978-1-57344-654-9 $14.95

The Sweetest Kiss
Ravishing Vampire Erotica
Edited by D. L. King

These sanguine tales give new meaning to the term "dead sexy" and feature beautiful bloodsuckers whose desires go far beyond blood.
ISBN 978-1-57344-371-5 $15.95

The Handsome Prince
Gay Erotic Romance
Edited by Neil Plakcy

A bawdy collection of bedtime stories brimming with classic fairy tale characters, reimagined and recast for any man who has dreamt of the day his prince will come. These sexy stories fuel fantasies and remind us all of the power of true romance.
ISBN 978-1-57344-659-4 $14.95

Daughters of Darkness
Lesbian Vampire Tales
Edited by Pam Keesey

"A tribute to the sexually aggressive woman and her archetypal roles, from nurturing goddess to dangerous predator."
—*The Advocate*
ISBN 978-1-57344-233-6 $14.95

Dark Angels
Lesbian Vampire Erotica
Edited by Pam Keesey

Dark Angels collects tales of lesbian vampires, the quintessential bad girls, archetypes of passion and terror. These tales of desire are so sharply erotic you'll swear you've been bitten!
ISBN 978-1-57344-252-7 $13.95

More of the Best Lesbian Erotica

Buy 4 books,
Get 1 *FREE**

Sometimes She Lets Me
Best Butch/Femme Erotica
Edited by Tristan Taormino

Does the swagger of a confident butch make you swoon?
Do your knees go weak when you see a femme straighten
her stockings? In *Sometimes She Lets Me*, Tristan Taormino
chooses her favorite butch/femme stories from the *Best
Lesbian Erotica* series.
ISBN 978-1-57344-382-1 $14.95

Lesbian Lust
Erotic Stories
Edited by Sacchi Green

Lust: It's the engine that drives us wild on
the way to getting us off, and lesbian lust
is the heart, soul and red-hot core of this
anthology.
ISBN 978-1-57344-403-3 $14.95

Girl Crush
Women's Erotic Fantasies
Edited by R. Gay

In the steamy stories of *Girl Crush,* women
satisfy their curiosity about the erotic possibilities of their infatuations.
ISBN 978-1-57344-394-4 $14.95

Girl Crazy
Coming Out Erotica
Edited by Sacchi Green

These irresistible stories of first times of all
kinds invite the reader to savor that delicious, dizzy feeling known as "girl crazy."
ISBN 978-1-57344-352-4 $14.95

Lesbian Cowboys
Erotic Adventures
Edited by Sacchi Green and Rakelle Va-
lencia

With stories that are edgy as shiny spurs
and tender as broken-in leather, fifteen
first-rate writers share their take on an
iconic fantasy.
ISBN 978-1-57344-361-6 $14.95

Essential Lesbian Erotica

The Harder She Comes
Butch / Femme Erotica
Edited by D. L. King

Some butches worship at the altar of their femmes, and many adorable girls long for the embrace of their suave, sexy daddies. In *The Harder She Comes*, we meet femmes who salivate at the sight of packed jeans and bois who dream of touching the corseted waist of a beautiful, confident woman.
ISBN 978-1-57344-778-2 $14.95

Girls Who Bite
Lesbian Vampire Erotica
Edited by Delilah Devlin

Whether depicting a traditional blood-drinker seducing a meal, a psychic vampire stealing the life force of an unknowing host, or a real-life sanguinarian seeking a partner to share a ritual bloodletting, the stories in *Girls Who Bite* are a sensual surprise.
ISBN 978-1-57344-715-7 $14.95

Girls Who Score
Hot Lesbian Erotica
Edited by Ily Goyanes

Girl jocks always manage to see a lot of action off the field. *Girls Who Score* is a winner, filled with story after story of competitive, intriguing women engaging in all kinds of contact sports.
ISBN 978-1-57344-825-3 $15.95

Wild Girls, Wild Nights
True Lesbian Sex Stories
Edited by Sacchi Green

Forget those fabled urban myths of lesbians who fill up U-Hauls on the second date and lead sweetly romantic lives of cocoa and comfy slippers. These are tales of wild women with dirty minds, untamed tongues and the occasional cuff or clamp. And they're all true!
ISBN 978-1-57344-933-5 $15.95

Stripped Down
Lesbian Sex Stories
Edited by Tristan Taormino

Where else but in a Tristan Taormino erotica collection can you find a femme vigilante, a virgin baby butch and a snake handler jostling for attention? The salacious stories in *Stripped Down* will draw you in and sweep you off your feet.
ISBN 978-1-57344-794-2 $15.95

Best Erotica Series

"Gets racier every year."—San Francisco Bay Guardian

Buy 4 books, Get 1 FREE*

Best Women's Erotica 2013
Edited by Violet Blue
ISBN 978-1-57344-898-7 $15.95

Best Women's Erotica 2012
Edited by Violet Blue
ISBN 978-1-57344-755-3 $15.95

Best Women's Erotica 2011
Edited by Violet Blue
ISBN 978-1-57344-423-1 $15.95

Best Bondage Erotica 2013
Edited by Rachel Kramer Bussel
ISBN 978-1-57344-897-0 $15.95

Best Bondage Erotica 2012
Edited by Rachel Kramer Bussel
ISBN 978-1-57344-754-6 $15.95

Best Bondage Erotica 2011
Edited by Rachel Kramer Bussel
ISBN 978-1-57344-426-2 $15.95

Best Lesbian Erotica 2013
Edited by Kathleen Warnock.
Selected and introduced by
Jewelle Gomez.
ISBN 978-1-57344-896-3 $15.95

Best Lesbian Erotica 2012
Edited by Kathleen Warnock.
Selected and introduced by
Sinclair Sexsmith.
ISBN 978-1-57344-752-2 $15.95

Best Lesbian Erotica 2011
Edited by Kathleen Warnock.
Selected and introduced by Lea DeLaria.
ISBN 978-1-57344-425-5 $15.95

Best Gay Erotica 2013
Edited by Richard Labonté.
Selected and introduced by Paul Russell.
ISBN 978-1-57344-895-6 $15.95

Best Gay Erotica 2012
Edited by Richard Labonté.
Selected and introduced by
Larry Duplechan.
ISBN 978-1-57344-753-9 $15.95

Best Gay Erotica 2011
Edited by Richard Labonté.
Selected and introduced by
Kevin Killian.
ISBN 978-1-57344-424-8 $15.95

Best Fetish Erotica
Edited by Cara Bruce
ISBN 978-1-57344-355-5 $15.95

Best Bisexual Women's Erotica
Edited by Cara Bruce
ISBN 978-1-57344-320-3 $15.95

Best Lesbian Bondage Erotica
Edited by Tristan Taormino
ISBN 978-1-57344-287-9 $16.95

* Free book of equal or lesser value. Shipping and applicable sales tax extra.
Cleis Press • (800) 780-2279 • orders@cleispress.com
www.cleispress.com

Ordering is easy! Call us toll free or fax us to place your MC/VISA order.
You can also mail the order form below with payment to:
Cleis Press, 2246 Sixth St., Berkeley, CA 94710.

ORDER FORM

QTY	TITLE	PRICE
____	_____	_____
____	_____	_____
____	_____	_____
____	_____	_____
____	_____	_____
____	_____	_____
____	_____	_____
____	_____	_____

SUBTOTAL _____

SHIPPING _____

SALES TAX _____

TOTAL _____

Add $3.95 postage/handling for the first book ordered and $1.00 for each additional book. Outside North America, please contact us for shipping rates. California residents add 9% sales tax. Payment in U.S. dollars only.

* Free book of equal or lesser value. Shipping and applicable sales tax extra.

Cleis Press • Phone: (800) 780–2279 • Fax: (510) 845–8001
orders@cleispress.com • www.cleispress.com
You'll find more great books on our website

Follow us on Twitter @cleispress • Friend/fan us on Facebook